INSTANT MENACE

INSTANT MENACE   9

TYNDALE HOUSE PUBLISHERS, INC., CAROL STREAM, ILLINOIS

RED ROCK MYSTERIES

#1 BEST-SELLING AUTHORS

JERRY B. JENKINS · CHRIS FABRY

Library of Congress Cataloging-in-Publication Data

Jenkins, Jerry B.
    Instant menace / Jerry B. Jenkins, Chris Fabry.
      p. cm. — (Red Rock mysteries ; 9) (Tyndale kids)
    Summary: When eighth grade begins, twins Ashley and Bryce get caught up in investigating why their principal left under mysterious circumstances, even as they struggle to get along with his replacement, who seems to be out to get them.
    ISBN-13: 978-1-4143-0148-8 (sc)
    ISBN-10: 1-4143-0148-0 (sc)
    [1. Schools —Fiction. 2. Online chat groups—Fiction. 3. Christian life—Fiction. 4. Twins —Fiction. 5. Colorado—Fiction. 6. Mystery and detective stories.] I. Fabry, Chris, date. II. Title. III. Series: Jenkins, Jerry B. Red Rock mysteries ; 9. IV. Series: Tyndale kids.
    PZ7.J4138Ins 2005
    [Fic]—dc22   2005021948

Printed in the United States of America

10 09 08 07 06
9   8   7   6   5   4   3   2   1

"In the end, we will **REMEMBER** not the words of our enemies, but the **SILENCE** of our friends."

Martin Luther King Jr.

"**EDUCATION** is the movement from darkness to **LIGHT**."

Allan Bloom

"You cannot get **AHEAD** while you are getting **EVEN**."

Dick Armey

CHAPTER 1

✖ Ashley ✖

The first day of school is a mixture of Christmas and a trip to the dentist. You want everyone to see your new clothes and you want to see your old friends and catch up on what's gone on over the summer, but there's also dread for what your teachers have in store.

The air is filled with the smell of fresh denim, sharpened pencils, and newly cleaned hallways. Immaculate backpacks swing behind pixies (our term for sixth graders), and you can almost feel their fear as they face their next three years.

Will the year be exciting? Will you get into the subjects and lose yourself, or will it be an educational root canal? I've had both experiences.

At least I had my twin brother to walk through the whole thing with me. His name is Bryce. We moved from Chicago a few years ago with our mom. Our dad died in a plane crash and she got remarried to Sam, a man whose wife and daughter died on the same plane. Wasn't my first choice, but I guess that's life. We have a little brother, Dylan, and a big stepsister, Leigh.

That Thursday morning, Leigh walked toward the bus stop with a face longer than a horse's. She'd been saving all summer to buy a car, and the long face was because she had to climb onto the yellow monster. She says there's nothing more humiliating than being a senior and riding the bus. Watching Bryce and me zoom away on our ATVs probably didn't help.

We motored to Mrs. Watson's barn, just across from the school. Eighth grade makes us kings and queens. No one older to bully us, and everyone younger looks up to us—or should. Other than our senior year in high school, this is the last time we'll have this feeling.

It felt like a long time since we had walked these halls. Summer is always too short, and ours had been full of adventure and mystery. Part of me looked forward to a nice, uneventful school year.

I saw my friend Hayley near my locker and we hugged. Bryce rolled his eyes and moved to first period. Marion Quidley waved and smiled. I'd come to know her a little better the past few weeks.

Duncan Swift tossed a football to Chuck Burly, and it bounced off Chuck's chin. Duncan is probably the best athlete and cutest guy in the school, but he doesn't pay much attention to me.

One of the best things about the first day is that teachers don't expect to accomplish much. You get your books, find out a little about your teachers and classmates, and go home. No big whoop.

I had great hopes for the year. I didn't see how anything could possibly go wrong, especially the first day.

But as soon as I stepped into Mrs. Sanchez's Spanish class, I thought I was going to throw up. Standing at the back window was none other than the school bully from last year, Boo Heckler.

CHAPTER 2

☻ *Bryce* ☻

First period I'm teacher's aide for Mr. Gminski, an English teacher who's also the forensics coach. Forensics is speech competition where people read dramatic stories or do duet or solo acting. I looked forward to the season, which starts in January.

I'd never been a teacher's aide, but it seemed fun. Mr. Gminski said I'd grade papers and be a gofer (go for this and go for that), or when there was nothing to do I could sack out behind his desk in the reading room.

The sixth graders filed in like lemmings jumping off a cliff. The guys all tried to look cool, strutting but laughing nervously. They looked so little that they reminded me of my brother, Dylan. It was his first day in kindergarten, and I couldn't wait to hear about that.

The bell rang and Mr. Gminski sauntered in. Short and stocky, he looks like a football linebacker with broad shoulders and a head too small for his neck. Reminds me of one of the comedians my Mom watched when she was young—the guy with the sunglasses and black suit.

Mr. Gminski told the class about where he'd taught before and what they'd do this year. Then he introduced me and asked me to call the roll and guess how to say all the names. But the intercom squawked, and the school secretary asked me to report to the front office.

"Uh-oh," one of the kids said.

CHAPTER 3

❀ Ashley ❀

Mrs. Sanchez had us stand until she called the roll and seated us, not alphabetically but by our new Spanish names. We got to choose from a list of first names and meanings. I wanted *Dolorita*, which means "full of sorrows," but I was afraid some people might think I was being morbid. Instead, I chose *Cristina*, which means "Christian," not so much because I wanted everyone to know I believed in God, but because Cristina Timberline sounds like a movie star's name.

I looked over the list for anything that meant "evil" or "frightens children with his fists" or "vandal," so my mouth nearly dropped to the floor when Boo picked *Fernando,* which means "brave." He'd been anything *but* brave with his toady little friend last year when they terrorized Bryce and me and the rest of the town. Boo had been sent to a juvenile detention facility because of his role in some vandalism in Red Rock, and Bryce and I had been the ones who figured out what had happened. I hoped Boo wouldn't find out we had cracked the case.

His real name is Aaron, but the whole school calls him Boo, because that's what he yells at every event. He boos when other teams are announced, boos the referees, and even boos at spelling bees. The name caught on among his victims—all of us—but we've never had the nerve to call him Boo to his face.

Since he's a year older, he's the size of most high schoolers. His hair is long in front and hangs over his eyes, and the back sticks up so he looks like an awkward chicken. His arms are gangly and his teeth crooked, with a thin film of green and big spaces between them. He has big knuckles and long, apelike fingers.

"Fernando, you sit there next to Cristina," Mrs. Sanchez said.

CHAPTER 4

◌ *Bryce* ◌

I strolled past the office fish tank and pecked on the glass,
letting the goldfish know I was back. Mrs. Mortenson, the secretary,
smiled the kind of smile you'd give a criminal heading for death row.
She shuffled papers. I looked at Mr. Forster's door.

"Go right in," she said. "He's expecting you."

Mr. Forster had made the transition to middle school a lot easier
for Ashley and me. He knew our dad had been killed and told us
he'd do anything he could to make our years at Red Rock Middle
School happy ones. Just remembering our names and saying hello in
the hallway was enough for me.

I stuck my head in the door and knocked politely.

Instead of Mr. Forster looking up, it was a different man. Glasses. Thinning hair over a shiny bald spot. Long nose. Crisp suit and tie.

"I'm sorry. I was looking for Mr. Forster."

He waved. "You must be Bryce. Come in and have a seat."

I looked back at Mrs. Mortenson, but she stared at the pile of papers. I sat. The nameplate on Mr. Forster's desk said *Miles Bookman.*

"I'm the new principal, getting acquainted with the students and faculty."

"What happened to Mr. Forster?"

He smiled, and that made his eyes shrink. "No longer with the school," he said, opening a black book. "I understand you have a twin, Mr. Timberline. Ashley?"

I nodded, dumbstruck.

"You and Ashley have been on the same team, attend many of the same classes?"

"Band and a few others, yeah."

He looked up. "Well, that simply will have to change. I'm moving you from the blue team to the red team. There's not much we can do about band, but other than that, you and your sister will be separated."

"But—"

"I assumed it would be easier for *you* to switch teams." He folded his hands on his desk. "Girls sometimes have a harder time making that transition, closer friendships and all. At least that's been my experience."

He made a few marks in the book, like ruining my entire life was as easy as putting a pen to the page.

CHAPTER 5

❀ Ashley ❀

"Remember me?" Fernando said. He gave me a green sneer.

I wondered if I could ever call him by his new name. He would always be Boo to me.

"Didn't think you'd have me for a classmate, did you, Timberline?"

"No," I said, acting as composed as I could. "I did hear you were—you'd be repeating eighth grade."

"They flunked me. Teachers are jerks." His face turned grim. "You and your brother still have those four-wheelers?"

Our major conflict with Boo had been over our ATVs and his

wanting to take them for a joyride one weekend. Bryce and I had stood firm, and I wondered if this year we'd have to do it again.

I pretended I didn't hear him and focused on Mrs. Sanchez. She has black hair and olive skin. Boo towers over her, but she has a quiet elegance I figured would overcome any bullying he might try.

The way Mrs. Sanchez pronounced our names made me almost want to change my citizenship. Mom had told me what a beautiful language Spanish was, and now I believed her. When Mrs. Sanchez rolled her *r*'s and said her vowels, I wanted to learn to speak the language just like she did.

"These people are going to wish they'd let me go on to high school," Boo said.

"I'm sure you're right."

"Fernando, let's begin with you," Mrs. Sanchez said. "Why did you choose Spanish as an elective?"

Boo shrugged. "Guessed I could pass the second time around. Plus, I figured you could help me learn how to pronounce stuff off the menu at Taco Bell." He laughed and looked around.

I heard a few snickers, but it didn't sound like people really thought it was funny. Mrs. Sanchez pursed her lips and moved on to others.

This is going to be a long year, I thought.

CHAPTER 6

☺ *Bryce* ☺

Instead of leaving, I lingered by the new principal's desk. He finally looked up, apparently surprised I was still there. "Yes?"

"When we came here, Mr. Forster said we could stay together because—"

"Mr. Forster is no longer the principal," Mr. Bookman said. "I've had to get up to speed on our student body quickly, and it's been no easy task."

He wiped his fingerprints from his expensive pen and slipped it into his breast pocket. "I've consulted numerous studies about twins in the same school. All indicate that separation is best and gives both students a better chance at academic and social success. Now, isn't that what we're all here for?"

I wasn't sure, because he talked so fast. "Yeah, I guess, but—"

"Then we understand each other." He checked his watch, then handed me a piece of paper. "This is your new class schedule. You'll be on the red team, as I said."

It made me mad that the man kept interrupting me. I don't like to judge people on just one meeting, but this guy was seriously going down on the friendly meter. The words he used, the way he talked down to me, and the way he looked—or didn't look—at me all made me think this was a man who didn't like kids. And if so, why was he our new principal?

"Where's Mr. Forster?" I said.

"I can't say."

"Will he be back?"

"That's to be determined." He took off his glasses. "Mr. Timberline, the past doesn't matter now. Whether Mr. Forster returns or not is irrelevant. What matters is the future, and that's why I'm here. I'm going to make this the very best setting for you and your sister to learn and grow and prepare for high school. Understood?"

I get suspicious when anyone tells me the past doesn't matter, because it does. I wanted to tell this guy how much Mr. Forster had helped us, how he too had probably looked at the charts and what the experts had to say, but he had cared enough to listen and find out what we thought.

"I guess," I said.

"I'm sure it will all work out, Mr. Timberline," he said, picking up the phone and turning from me. "You'll thank me for this one day."

Mrs. Mortenson gave me one of those I'm-really-sorry smiles as I passed her on the way out.

"Oh, one more thing," the principal said, coming to the door. "I know the previous administration looked the other way about this, but I'm aware that you ride to school on all-terrain vehicles. That needs to stop as of today."

"What?"

"You can drive them home after school, but tomorrow ride the bus, walk, or have your parents bring you."

CHAPTER 7

❀ Ashley ❀

I couldn't wait to tell Bryce all about Boo, but when I got to band, he looked like someone had smashed his Little Debbie cake. (Bryce likes the oatmeal cream pies.) He stood with the rest of the percussion guys—a weird group, if you ask me—and stared at the xylophone.

Some people say you can sense what your twin is thinking, but neither Bryce nor I believe that. There is a special bond between us, but I think it's because we spend a lot of time together solving mysteries instead of some swimming-in-the-womb-together ability.

"What's wrong?" I said.

He told me in one long sentence, which Mr. Gminski would have corrected because it was a run-on. Then he handed me his schedule. Other than band, we were separated the whole day.

"And that's not the worst of it," Bryce said. "The new guy says we can't ride our ATVs to school anymore."

"What? We don't even park on school grounds!"

"Doesn't matter. And you can bet he'll be outside waiting for us tomorrow morning."

Mr. Scarberry, our band teacher, walked in with his patented cup of coffee. We all thought it was probably superglued to his hand. I went back to the flute section but kept glancing at Bryce. We squabbled like typical siblings, but recently we had gotten through some rough years together. Now it felt like we were being torn apart at the seams. I stared at "Shaker Variants," a piece we had played last year, trying to hit the notes and remembering messing it up during our spring performance.

I stopped playing when I thought about losing my ATV. Now I knew how Leigh felt about not having a car.

CHAPTER 8

◒ *Bryce* ◒

I trudged into science class, and everyone looked at me like I had a huge target on my back. I'd been on the blue team the last two years, and though I knew the names of most of these people, I didn't know many well.

Mr. Blunt looked over the class list and scowled at me.

I showed him my changed schedule and told him the new principal had separated Ashley and me. "What happened to Mr. Forster?"

Mr. Blunt furrowed his brow and his eyes wandered. "Nothing I can tell you. He left only a few days ago."

Mr. Blunt killed most of our class time talking about baseball and handing out books. It was okay with me because I like baseball and was looking forward to the Cubs playing in Colorado.

The conversation turned toward actual science and some recent discoveries of dinosaur fossils in Wyoming. I usually keep my mouth shut in strange groups, but I raised my hand. "No wonder they became extinct. There's nothing in Wyoming."

A few people chuckled. Then a girl in the corner raised her hand. She had long, silky black hair that reflected the fluorescent lights. Big eyes. Lips as red as the *C* on a Cubs jersey. Milky white skin with a few cute freckles. Basically a 15 on a scale of 1 to 10.

"I'm from Wyoming, and there's a lot more there than people think," she said, staring at me.

"Ouch," somebody whispered.

Mr. Blunt looked over his sheet. "It's Lynette, isn't it? Lynette Jarvis?"

She nodded. "Just moved here."

"What brings you to Colorado?"

"We had to sell because there was so much drilling. My dad didn't know somebody else owned the mineral rights on our property. That meant the drillers could come anytime they wanted. We moved there to get away from all the pollution. It's really pretty." She stared daggers at me.

"So, what do you think of the fossil findings, Lynette?" Mr. Blunt said.

She shrugged. "What I still don't get are these crazy people who believe in fairy tales."

"Explain."

"You know, people who ignore the evidence, the fossil record, real science. They say God created everything, and a big boat carried all the animals, that kind of thing. It's just silly."

The class fell silent until a guy behind me said, "Religion's a crutch for people who don't want to use their brains."

"Yeah," another said. "There've been more wars started in the name of God than anything else."

I was suddenly feeling like a stranger in my own school, and my face burned. I wanted to say something snappy that would really put these people in their places, defend God, stand up for my beliefs.

But I just sat there staring at the black-haired girl, wishing I hadn't said anything about Wyoming.

CHAPTER 9

❋ Ashley ❋

It wasn't that I needed Bryce beside me all the time. It was just nice after losing my real dad to have somebody I could lean on, trust in, and know would understand.

Mrs. Ferguson asked us to use the first class in language arts to write an essay. Everybody groaned, but I love to write and was glad to have something to do.

"Speed-write about something that happened over the summer," Mrs. Ferguson said. "Pick something that taught you a lesson about yourself."

Chuck Burly sat looking confused, mirroring just about everyone's face but mine. I could think of about a million things I'd learned. We'd taken care of a neighbor's alpaca farm, helped a friend realize a huge goal, solved a mystery of someone trying to sabotage the local country club, and a lot more.

While everyone else asked Mrs. Ferguson to explain more about the assignment, I started writing, letting the words flow and not worrying about making everything perfect.

> *I learned a lot about myself and my family during a trip to the Grand Canyon this summer. I wasn't expecting to get dehydrated, run out of water, almost die, and escape from a criminal. Hiking into the canyon in 120-degree heat and going through that makes it easy to live through a math or history exam and even the Colorado Aptitude Tests.*
>
> *I also learned how much I take for granted at home. Running water. Clean bathrooms. Fresh food. Sidewalks free of mule poop. Refrigerators. Arby's shakes. It's a gift to crawl into bed and not have to worry about waking up to scorpions or rattlesnakes.*
>
> *And most of all, I learned again that I can depend on God. He's there when I ask for help, waiting for me to call on him. I wish all my friends could discover the ways God can help during hard times.*

I hadn't intended to write about God on my first day in class—it just kind of slipped out. I wondered what Mrs. Ferguson would think. Some Christians try to write every paper about God, Jesus, or the Bible. I'm not saying they're wrong, but Mom says you need to find your own style.

CHAPTER 10

☻ *Bryce* ☻

Academic enrichment is what they call it now, but it used to be homeroom. The teacher tries to get us ready for the next round of tests from the state—I guess so they can prove they're doing their jobs. But the first day is pretty fun because they try to build teamwork and figure out how to bolster school spirit.

Except I was now on the red team. I'd been building school spirit for the blue team for two whole years, trying to figure out ways to make us better, and now I was on the side of the enemy.

I was lucky to have at least one good friend in the class: Kael Barnes. I explained what had happened, but he seemed wary of me.

The usual suggestions about building the team went around, and it was eerie how much like the blue team this was. People suggested bake sales or car washes. Another wanted to have a day where we all wore red, or a nonblue dance where we wouldn't wear anything blue and would stand around the cafeteria and listen to music because we're all too scared to actually dance.

One girl suggested we do something to help the victims of the latest natural disaster, a hurricane, and I thought that was pretty good. Someone else suggested we raise money to build a plaque with people's names on it, but it wasn't clear whose names. I suggested "Red student of the week," but nobody laughed except the kid next to me, Harris. He'd moved to Red Rock the year before, and I hadn't heard him say more than "Please pass the salt" in all that time.

Lynette, the black-haired dream girl, raised a hand. "I wonder if we're doing all we can for the environment. Recycling, for instance. I see a lot of empty blue containers around school, and the trash cans are filled with soda cans."

Mrs. Hyre wrote the idea on the board and asked for more. I wanted to mention my efforts to fight global warming to impress Lynette, but I guessed taking my socks off every night wouldn't qualify.

Finally, Kael said, "Our school has a Web page for each team, but they're pretty lame. You know, test results, grades, a calendar for sporting events."

"What's wrong with that?" Mrs. Hyre said.

"Nothing, but it's just information. What if we could make the site even better?"

"I'm listening," she said.

Kael sat up and the class got quiet. "One of the problems is that some participate and others don't. Not everybody is comfortable talking. But if you could make suggestions or point out problems without anybody knowing who you were, more would get involved. And everyone's comments would have equal value because you're not thinking, 'Oh, that's a basketball player' or 'That guy's a nerd.' Shy kids would feel freer to talk using the computer. Kids who always talk will have to listen for a change."

"So what do we do—write notes and pass a hat?" someone said.

"No. We'll have a Web site and include a chat room. Instant Messenger. That type of thing. We'll call it the Red Room."

Mrs. Hyre had her hand on her chin. "I don't know. I've heard those things are kind of dangerous. People outside the group can get in. I don't let my kids use Instant Messenger."

"Yeah, and it's easy for fights to start," Carlos said.

"No one will be able to get in but us," Kael said. Then he looked at me. "If we can keep it a secret from the blue team."

CHAPTER 11

❁ Ashley ❁

I found Bryce at lunch. We were both bummed about the ATVs. I could have a terrible day, flunk a test, lose a friend, whatever, and still look forward to riding home.

Marion Quidley sat beside us and eyed Bryce while she pulled out a bean-sprout-and-alfalfa sandwich—at least that's what it looked like. "Heard you were on the red team now. Why'd you defect?"

"Wasn't my idea," Bryce said.

I explained. "But if we can get Mr. Forster back we'll solve the whole thing."

Most around the table hadn't heard Mr. Forster was gone. Of

course, Marion had. She's known for her wild theories about space aliens and Bigfoot sightings, but she also has a bead on the latest gossip.

"I heard Mr. Forster was caught embezzling money and they fired him," Marion said.

"Embezzling?" I said.

"Fancy word for stealing," Marion said. "Crunching numbers. Cooking the books. It happens."

"I can't imagine Mr. Forster doing that," Bryce said.

"After what he wrote in the local paper about the school superintendent?" Marion said. "I'd believe anything."

"I don't remember that," I said.

Marion munched a carrot. "I think it came out the week you guys were on vacation. I didn't actually read it, but I heard he ripped on the superintendent. School policies and stuff like that."

"That doesn't sound like Mr. Forster," I said.

Marion shrugged. "Maybe he's under stress opening a new business."

We both stared at her.

"You haven't heard?" she said, waving her carrot like a magic wand. "He and his wife rented that old library building in town. They're turning it into a bookstore and juice bar."

"How do you know all this?" Bryce said.

"I can't help it if you guys are out of the loop."

Bryce and I finished our lunch and rushed to the school library before our next class. I love the scent of that place—the books, magazines, and newspapers smell like knowledge.

We found the back issues of the local paper and opened the one printed the week we were gone. On the Letters to the Editor page, Mr. Forster's was titled "Miffed at Super."

*If the people of Red Rock knew the true story of what's
going on behind the scenes at our schools, they'd be
outraged. The superintendent is incompetent and lazy,
and he puts the needs of the students last, instead of first.*

The letter went on to accuse the superintendent of other things,
including "lying at school-board meetings," and called for the man
to be fired.

It was signed *Thomas Forster, Principal, Red Rock Middle
School.*

CHAPTER 12

☺ *Bryce* ☺

Ashley and I walked into town after school to look for Mr. or Mrs. Forster at the old library. Several older buildings had been rebuilt into small shops and restaurants. The downtown was making a comeback. On Saturdays in the summer a farmers' market sold fresh corn, tomatoes, cucumbers, and other vegetables in the streets.

Flags flapped outside the wooden and brick buildings. Some had Red Rock written on them. Others said Open or Sale. Johnny's Pawn and Deli stood at the end of the row and was the only one with a neon sign.

The old library was an L-shaped brick building, and I could imagine

kids 50 years ago lining up to check out Dr. Seuss books. Black garbage bags covered the windows, and a handwritten sign on the door
read Opening Soon.

We knocked, but no one answered. Then I noticed the school-
district building a couple of blocks away. It stood like a red monster
against the front range of mountains. The windows actually made it
look like a jack-o'-lantern.

"Someone in there will know where Mr. Forster is," I said.

We'd gotten to the building's parking lot when my phone war-
bled. (Ashley doesn't have one because she doesn't like spending
the money.)

"I need you two home quick," Sam said.

CHAPTER 13

✖ Ashley ✖

We raced back to our ATVs and sped home.

Sam stood waiting, his mustache curved over his lip and his hands thrust in his jeans pockets, as we parked near the barn. His office is upstairs, and the downstairs is a barn in name only. We don't have any smelly animals. Sam is a charter pilot, so sometimes he's gone for a couple of days, or he might be around all week.

"Need your help," Sam said. He opened the barn door and I gasped. Inside was an old, gold, dented Honda Accord Leigh had test-driven the week before, but she had been about $300 short of the asking price.

"You got it!" Bryce said.

Sam smiled. "Waiting a week made him come down in price. I took it by the electronics store, and they installed a radio that'll play her MP3 collection."

The windshield was cracked, as were a couple of hubcaps, and I noticed cigarette burns on the backseat. But no doubt Leigh would see this as a gleaming chariot.

"Help me with the bow," Sam said.

I grabbed a roll of duct tape and helped him secure a huge red bow on the roof of the car.

"I called Randy and asked him to stall Leigh," he said.

"She's going to freak out," I said.

"Help me string her along when she gets here. Bryce, start the video camera when she gets home. This ought to be priceless."

CHAPTER 14

⊌ *Bryce* ⊌

Mom had a big smile as we moved inside. "Randy just called. He wanted to know if we were ready."

We spent a few minutes listening to Dylan describe kindergarten. He acted like the whole thing was the most important experience of his life. He told us about his classmates and described his teacher and their room. The whole thing was a hoot, and I had a hard time not laughing. Of course, as I thought about it, it *was* the biggest event in his life.

As soon as Leigh walked through the door I could tell Randy had done a good job of setting her up. She glared at Sam. "'Course I had to beg for a ride or take the big yellow bus, thanks to you and your just-wait-and-the-seller-will-come-down philosophy."

I held the video camera by my side and caught the whole thing. Mom had to turn away to keep from laughing out loud.

"I'm fine with you getting a car," Sam said, "but I really don't think you can afford to borrow the extra over what you already have."

"Come on, Dad. I was only a few hundred dollars away from the Honda."

Sam sighed. "Why don't you call the guy and find out if he'll take less?"

"He already said no."

"Never hurts to ask. Maybe he's getting antsy to sell."

"I can really call him?"

"Sure."

I kept the camera going as Leigh dialed. Her shoulders slumped and she banged the phone down. "He sold it this afternoon! This is your fault!"

"Why don't you look in the newspaper?" Sam said. "There have to be new listings."

"I can take you to look tonight," Randy said.

Through clenched teeth Leigh said, "Where's the paper?"

"In the recycle bin in the barn," Mom said.

Leigh stomped out the back door. Even Pippin and Frodo seemed to know what was up, yipping and nipping at Leigh's pants as she moved like a steam engine toward the barn.

I followed as close as I dared, with the camera running.

When she opened the barn door, she headed straight for the recycle bin, not even noticing the car. I couldn't believe it. She riffled through the newspapers, then turned to see us all standing at the door. "I can't find it!" she said to Mom.

"You don't need it," Randy said.

She looked from face to face, then saw the video camera. A look of confusion came over her, and she slowly turned. The picture could not have been framed better. She was right in front of the car, the red ribbon next to her face. It almost looked like the car was smiling at her.

She bent forward, her mouth dropped open, and she clamped her hands over her face and squealed. "But . . . the guy said . . . you mean . . . how did you . . . when . . . ?"

Finally she screamed, "Dad!" and jumped on Sam and threw her arms around him. Mom hugged both of them.

Leigh hopped inside the car, squealing again when she saw the new radio. She squealed louder when she heard what Sam had paid for it.

"Did you know about this, Randy?" she said.

He nodded and she whacked him on the shoulder. She stared at me and grinned. "Turn that thing off!"

CHAPTER 15

❀ Ashley ❀

Leigh brought home a bag full of stuff for her car. New floor covering, an air freshener to hang from her rearview mirror, a bobblehead dog for the back, and a couple of Red Rock High School bumper stickers. In a state of sisterly euphoria, she offered to swing by the coffee shop the next morning, buy Bryce and me Frappuccinos, and drop us off at school. That solved our ATV dilemma for one day.

Mom asked what had happened at school, and I gave her the nothing-much routine. "Mr. Forster wasn't there. You haven't heard anything about him, have you?"

She furrowed her brow. "No. I'll have to ask at the next Moms in Touch prayer meeting."

Leigh was as excited as I'd ever seen her Friday morning.

Bryce and I got our Frappuccinos, and as she drove past the old library, I pointed out to Bryce that the windows no longer had garbage bags.

When Leigh dropped us off, Mr. Bookman was standing outside. "Mr. and Miss Timberline, thank you for your cooperation."

Bryce waved as he took a long sip of his drink.

Mr. Bookman held up a hand as we were about to walk inside. "You know that's not allowed, don't you?"

"Our sister driving us?" Bryce said.

"No, those drinks. You can't take them inside."

We'd been drinking Frappuccinos the past two years, and our teachers in first period even let us bring them to class. Snacks too.

"When did that rule start?" Bryce said.

"It's in the student handbook. Why don't you familiarize yourself with it?" Mr. Bookman nodded toward the trash can, where two kids with brain freeze were shivering, moaning, holding their heads, and trying to finish their drinks.

"We have to get Mr. Forster back," Bryce muttered as our cups splashed into the can.

☺ *Bryce* ☺

Every teacher I asked about Mr. Forster had the same response—a tight-lipped shake of the head and "I'm sorry. I can't say anything."

I even asked our janitor, Mr. Patterson, the nicest person in the whole school. He just stared at me. "Mr. Forster's not working here anymore? I saw him the day before yesterday."

"Where?"

"Down at Ms. Prine's room."

In academic enrichment, when Mrs. Hyre stepped out of the room for a second, Kael stood. "Listen, everybody, I've talked with kids from the rest of the team, and they like our Instant Messenger idea. But there's no way the teachers and administrators are going to approve it."

"Yeah," Carlos said, "they won't even let us bring drinks in anymore."

"Anyway," Kael continued, "I set up a Red Room on the Web last night. You have to have the password and an approved screen name to get in."

He told us to make up a goofy name, write it on a scrap of paper, and give it to him after class. "Don't tell anyone your screen name, and fold it so I won't see it either. Tomorrow I'll give everybody the password, and we'll try this puppy out."

Lynette had on a shirt as red as a fire engine, which made her black hair even more striking. I flashed her my best I'm-sorry-we've-had-problems-can't-we-try-again? smile.

She flashed me an I-don't-speak-to-roadkill smirk.

I tore a piece of paper in half and sat thinking of a good screen name. It had to be something no one could pin on me. I love bacon, lettuce, and tomato sandwiches and Michael Jordan (even though I've only seen videos of him), so I wrote *BLT23*, folded it, and tossed it to Kael.

CHAPTER 17

❀ Ashley ❀

Ms. Prine is the blue team's science teacher. She's single, and we've been trying to get her married to Mr. Blunt since sixth grade. But there doesn't seem to be much chemistry there, pardon the pun.

It turns out the person who likes her the most is Boo Heckler. He sat up when she walked into the room, chuckled, and said, "I like your dress, purty teacher."

She stared at him and dipped her head. "I thought we had an understanding about this, Aaron. Do we need to go to the office and walk through it again?"

"No, ma'am." Boo covered his mouth and laughed.

Ms. Prine is really into archaeology and digging up artifacts. Every year she shows us the coins she once discovered on a college expedition. Getting her into that story can take up half a class period if you ask the right questions. Once we even delayed a test a whole day by getting her to talk about that memory.

She was handing out our books and having us cut up paper bags as book covers when the coin subject came up again. She got that familiar gleam in her eyes.

I'd heard the story 50 times—the way her team separated in the countryside, how she chose a place to dig, and what it was like when she uncovered the coins. The people on her team thought her find was good but nothing to be excited about. Then she had the coins appraised and found out they were worth several thousand dollars.

"Let's see them," Hayley said. "Maybe some of that good luck will rub off on us."

"You want to see them? Really?" Ms. Prine unlocked a wooden cabinet in the corner. She moved beakers and other equipment and frantically pushed papers to the side. She opened both doors, bent over, stood on her tiptoes and eyed the top shelf, then hurried out of the room.

◑ *Bryce* ◑

Ashley found me at my locker before final period and said
we had to talk. "Looks like we have another mystery," she said.
"Tell you after school."

In last period, Kael told me he had signed up almost everyone on
the team for the Red Room. "I'm sending the password to about 20
people through regular e-mail so we can do a test run. You in?"

"Sure."

After the final bell I found Ashley, and she said Ms. Prine's coins
were missing. "She told me after class that there are only two keys to

the cabinet. She has one and Mr. Forster had the other. He put it in her mailbox before he left."

"Any idea when the coins were taken?"

"Ms. Prine said the last time she saw them was at the end of last year."

"She left them over the summer?"

"They were locked up. Mr. Bookman called the police."

My stomach clenched. "Ash, the janitor said he saw Mr. Forster here before school started, near Ms. Prine's room."

"C'mon, Bryce. You don't think—"

"I can't imagine him *ever* doing something like that."

Our bus had already left, and we wanted to walk to town anyway. The old library had a sign out front that read Juicy Pages. Sounded quirky, but I knew people would sit and read while they sipped a juice drink. The inside was dark, though.

"Let's check at the administration building," Ashley said. "We never got the chance to ask inside the other day."

The building used to be a school, but I didn't expect it to be so big. The ceilings were 20 feet high. I could have shot a three-pointer in the lobby.

A woman looked up from her computer. When I said we were trying to find Mr. Forster, she raised her eyebrows and punched a couple of buttons on her phone. "No answer," she said, cradling the phone between her shoulder and ear. "He was here earlier. Might be in the restroom."

I looked at Ashley with wide eyes. We'd stumbled onto his hiding place.

The woman punched a couple more buttons. "Mary, have you seen Tom? I see. . . ." She hung up. "He was called to the middle school. You just missed him."

CHAPTER 19

✾ Ashley ✾

I'd been keeping a secret from Bryce, and it had nothing to do with the stolen coins. Someone on the blue team had heard about a Web site chat room the red team had created, and Hayley asked me to get information about it from Bryce. She figured since he had just gone to the new team, he wouldn't feel as loyal to them and might be coming back to the blue team as soon as Mr. Forster returned anyway.

I was being asked to spy on my own brother, which I didn't like. As we left the administration building, I wondered whether to tell him.

A gray-haired man with a briefcase came out a side exit and strode through the parking lot. "Isn't that Dr. Mauban, the superintendent?" I said. He'd attended some of our band concerts, and of course his picture was often in the paper. Mom said he had the most thankless job in the state.

He was whistling a tune from a musical. A lot of adults walk past kids without even looking up. I think they pretend you're not there. But Dr. Mauban looked right at us and smiled, then kept whistling as he reached his car.

"You're Dr. Mauban, aren't you?" I said.

"Why, yes." He set his briefcase down. "And you are?"

I introduced us.

Dr. Mauban shook our hands. "What brings you two to our neck of the woods?"

"We came looking for Mr. Forster," Bryce said. "We really miss him at the middle school."

Dr. Mauban nodded.

"Do you know why he's not working there anymore?" I said.

He kept nodding, then looked at the ground and pawed at it with a foot. "I'm afraid I do. I wish I could talk to you about it, but . . ."

"Is it about the letter in the newspaper?" I said.

"No, no. Tom says he didn't even write that, and I believe him. There are other issues I can't talk about that need to be ironed out. It'll all be dealt with at the board meeting."

"Will he be back at the middle school this year?" Bryce said.

"I don't know." He smiled. "I'm afraid I just can't talk about it."

As Dr. Mauban drove away, I looked at Bryce. "Is it possible Mr. Forster isn't who we thought he was?"

CHAPTER 20

☾ *Bryce* ☾

That night, sitting at the computer, I got Kael's e-mail, which included my password. *And no telling that blue-team sister of yours,* he added.

I'm shocked you'd even think it, I typed back.

I found the Red Room and logged on. At least 20 people were sailing messages back and forth. I gave up trying to figure out who was attached to each weird name. Greenboy21. Lollapawinner88. Schwinnsterama123. I thought by reading the messages I could figure out who was who, but no.

Baileywickzzz: Hear about the big heist today?
Lollapawinner88: Somebody take Patterson's favorite mop?
Greenboy21: Coach Baldwin missing some athletic supporters?
Baileywickzzz: No, Ms. Prine's coin collection's gone. They even called Mr. Forster in. Saw him there after school.
Greenboy21: He probably sold the coins to pay his gambling debt.
Cabooseontheloose: Didn't know he gambled.
Greenboy21: That's why he was kicked out of school.
Lollapawinner88: I heard he was addicted to painkillers.
ChangesMade44: Boo probably did it.

I was beginning to see why Mrs. Hyre thought this might not be a good idea. Instead of bringing the team together and helping those who were too intimidated to speak up, this was just a big gossip fest.

PingPongU: Who's Mr. Forster?

I stared at the message. The only new kid on the red team was Lynette, the black-haired beauty. I pulled up the dialog box and typed a message.

BLT23: Forster is one of the nicest guys on the planet. Helped us when we first moved here. Used to be our principal.
PingPongU: I don't get sent to the office much. I wouldn't know. :)

I smiled, thinking of Lynette sitting alone, watching the words whiz by. Maybe if I could impress her through the computer without her knowing who I was I could get a chance to change her mind about God and all of that stuff.

Then I imagined us together in high school, going on a date, me driving us to the prom or maybe a movie.

"What's going on?" Ashley said as she walked into the living room.

I almost fell out of my chair. I covered the screen with my hands and said, "Nothing. Don't."

"Don't what? I just walked in and—"

"Just don't do it again. You almost gave me a heart attack."

She stared at the colored background between my fingers. "Is that a chat room?"

"It's for school. Now do you mind?"

Ashley shrugged and walked away. "Fine. You want to keep secrets, keep secrets."

When I uncovered the screen, people were on to theories about who might have stolen the coins.

> **Cabooseontheloose: Patterson has to have a key to that cabinet.**
> **BLT23: He doesn't.**
> **Greenboy21: How do you know?**

Good question. I shouldn't have sounded so sure.

> **BLT23: Just heard there were only two keys.**
> **Greenboy21: Don't believe everything you hear. I think it's somebody from that church that meets there on Sundays.**
> **BLT23: Classrooms are locked, aren't they?**
> **Greenboy21: They open some for the nursery and kids classes.**

PingPongU: Figures—church people are all hypos if you ask me.
Schwinnsterama123: Hypos? I go to that church and I've never seen any hippos there. :)
PingPongU: LOL.

PingPongU had to be Lynette, but who was Schwinnsterama123?

CHAPTER 21

❀ Ashley ❀

What were Bryce and the others talking about in their secret chat room? What kinds of team building were they doing?

"Ready, Ashley?" Mom said, and I jumped. Now I knew how Bryce felt when I startled him.

"Your counseling appointment," she said. "It was rescheduled for today. You're going to be late."

Bryce and I started going to a counselor at church soon after Mom became a Christian. She thought it would help us deal with my dad's death, and at first I dreaded it. Now I really like seeing Mrs. Ogilvie. She helps me work through feelings and stuff at school.

One of her best ideas was for me to start writing a journal. I light my scented candle, burrow under the covers, and write whatever comes to mind. Sometimes I'll write for a whole hour and forget I'm even writing. Stuff just seems to come out.

Mrs. Ogilvie's office has a gorgeous view of Pikes Peak. The sun was shining through when I got there, and she pulled the shade so I wouldn't squint.

I hadn't seen her since before summer vacation, so there was a lot to talk about. Eventually I brought up Mr. Forster and how much Bryce and I missed him. She listened closely and asked questions about the new principal. I wondered if she knew more about the situation than she was letting on.

"Have you thought about what you'll do if Mr. Forster never comes back?" she said. "How would you feel if the days of riding your ATV to school are over?"

"Bryce and I love it, but I guess I'd be okay. I mean, nobody's going to die because we don't get to ride our ATVs."

She laced her fingers like the old "Here's the church—here's the steeple" rhyme. "Losing things reveals something about each of us. You've seen that with your father. How we respond to that loss says a lot more about us than we realize."

"Like what?"

"I once heard a pastor say, 'Not wanting something is better than having it.' In other words, if you think you have to have a certain type of bike or toy or dress, it has some control over you. You can't live without it. But if you look at that bike or toy or dress and realize you don't *have* to have it, it loses its power. Then if you get it, it's fine, but if you don't, it's fine too."

"What does that have to do with Mr. Forster?"

Mrs. Ogilvie leaned back in her chair. "People make mistakes, and they'll let you down. Do you have to have Mr. Forster at your school to be happy?"

"Do you know something about him that we don't?"

She lifted her eyebrows and just stared at me.

CHAPTER 22

☺ *Bryce* ☺

Ashley and I never look for mysteries—they just seem to find us. Plenty of times we thought something was going to be a mystery, and it turned into nothing. But this was different. Mr. Forster was in trouble, and whether or not he was guilty of stealing the coins or whatever else they'd accused him of, we had to get to the bottom of it.

I hopped on my ATV and headed for an office building not far from the gymnasium where I sometimes practice basketball. In the phone book I'd found the name of the church that met at our school and it listed this address, so I figured it would be better to show up in person than to call.

I recognized the lady at the front desk of The Flock offices as a mother who'd chaperoned our band trip to Happy Canyons amusement park a few months before. She recognized me too and called me by name.

I asked her all about the church. They had been meeting at our school for more than a year, had almost 200 regular attendees, and had bought land east of Red Rock. They hoped to move into their own building within a year.

"What rooms do you guys use in the school?" I said.

"The cafeteria is where we worship. We use the lobby to welcome people."

"What about Sunday school and the nursery?" I said.

"We use several classrooms upstairs for adult classes. Kids' classes are in the sixth-grade section. The nursery is farther down—I think in a couple of the eighth-grade classrooms." She paused. "Can I ask what this is about?"

"Just curious," I said. "The nursery—do you know which room that's in?"

"The infants are in the library. And the toddler nursery is in one of the science rooms."

"Are there volunteers for the toddlers? I mean, you don't pay people to come in and babysit, right?"

"It's all volunteer," she said.

"Would I be able to see a list of volunteers?"

"Oh no. I wouldn't be comfortable about doing that unless I knew what you—"

Someone came in and a radio squawked. A police officer.

"May I help you?" the woman said.

The officer glanced at me and looked around the room. "I need to talk with the pastor and whoever schedules your volunteers at the school."

The secretary gave me a that's-a-coincidence look. When she went to get the pastor, I grabbed my helmet and left.

CHAPTER 23

Ashley

Bryce's report didn't clear Mr. Forster, but it did give us more suspects. One thing about mysteries: you have to think of all the angles.

"What if Ms. Prine is behind this?" Bryce said Saturday afternoon as we chatted in my room. "Maybe she needed the cash and sold the coins. Why else would she store them where everybody knew where they were except to make it look like someone took them?"

"Selling your own coins is no crime," I said. "Unless she wanted the cash for them, *and* she wanted to claim some insurance for them as if they were lost or stolen. But I saw the look on her face when she found them missing. If she sold them, she deserves an Academy Award. Plus, wouldn't she feel bad if she did it and the blame somehow shifted to Mr. Forster?"

Bryce shook his head. "He's the only one who can clear this up."

I called information and got Mr. Forster's number for Bryce. Bryce dialed, listened a few seconds, then hung up. "Disconnected. No new number available."

CHAPTER 24

☺ *Bryce* ☺

It was overcast Monday morning, and neither Ashley nor I felt like walking to school. Leigh had already left, so we headed to the bus stop. Back in Illinois we had lived so close to school that we walked every day. I miss those days of walking hand in hand with my dad to after-school stuff. Climbing into the bus made me remember why I liked riding my ATV so much. Freedom. Controlling your own schedule. No rowdy kids throwing gum.

I sat behind Marion Quidley. I wouldn't have, but it was the only seat open.

"Saw your posts last night, Timberline," she said, not turning around.

That sent a shiver through me. Had I talked with Marion? Had Ashley seen my screen name and told her? Our posts were supposed to be anonymous. She had to be guessing, fishing for information. "How do you know it was me?"

Marion turned and smiled. "I can just tell." She leaned closer. "Don't worry—your secret is safe with me, BLT."

No way was I going to give her the satisfaction of knowing she had figured it out. And I vowed I wasn't going to change my screen name either.

Later Kael handed a sheet of paper to everyone in class and had a stack as tall as a Big Mac to give to other classes. "The site worked even better than I figured. Almost everybody jumped in, and it got really interesting. Lots of guesses about Mr. Forster."

"What kind of guesses?" I said.

"About why they fired him. Somebody said they thought he'd been arrested for drunk driving. Another said he smuggled money out of the school to start his store."

"That wasn't what this site was supposed to be about."

"Hey, when people try to keep secrets we have to guess, right? Plus, we have freedom of speech."

I stuffed the sheet in my pocket and bit the inside of my cheek.

I guess Kael could tell I was upset because he put a hand on my shoulder. "Look, Forster might turn out to be a crook, and if he is, you'll read it first in the Red Room. If he's not, you'll read it there too."

By now the whole school had heard about Ms. Prine's missing coins. A lot of kids suspected Boo Heckler, though there was no evidence against him. I wondered if Boo's trip to the juvenile facility had changed him or if he'd start bullying people like last year.

As the day wore on, people talked more about Mr. Forster.

Rumors ranged from his cheating on the CATs—the Colorado Apti-
tude Tests—to his stealing gas from buses.

Mr. Bookman watched the lunchroom like a hawk, waiting for
someone to toss a food wrapper on the floor or not finish their milk,
I guess. I found Ashley and learned she'd heard the rumors too.

"As soon as the bell rings, we're at the administration building,"
I said.

CHAPTER 25

❀ Ashley ❀

Bryce and I shielded our eyes against a stiff wind that blew dust and trash into our faces. The weather can change quickly when the elevation is over 7,000 feet.

The secretary at the administration building was on the phone, but she held up a hand for us to wait. "He's up there," she said finally, pointing us toward the stairs.

Mr. Forster's office was on the third floor, and the view from the huge window at the top of the stairs was dizzying.

He met us in the hall and showed us to his desk. I'd never seen him without a tie, so it was shocking to see him in an open-collared shirt.

"How have you two been?" he said as we all sat in his office. "Have a good summer?"

Bryce told him about our adventure in the Grand Canyon but quickly changed the subject. "We were really surprised and disappointed you weren't at school."

Mr. Forster rubbed his hands on his pants. "I miss it. And if I could be there, believe me, I would."

"What happened?" I said.

He stared at me like I'd asked the million-dollar question. "I wish I could go into it. The hardest thing about this is that I can't defend myself."

"Rumors are flying that you stole stuff, that you were caught by the police and—"

"That's not true." He lowered his voice. "I was accused of writing a letter to the editor, which I never did. Whoever did it used letterhead from the school and forged my signature."

"We've read the letter," Bryce said, "but they wouldn't have put you on leave for that."

He nodded. "The superintendent is a good man. But when the allegation came in—an anonymous call about my misappropriating funds—"

"What does that mean?" Bryce said.

"Stealing," he said. "But I've said too much already."

"So there's money missing," Bryce said, "and on top of that, the coins—"

"You know about Ms. Prine's collection?" Mr. Forster shook his head. "I was the only other one who had a key to that cabinet. Someone has stolen those coins and accused me, but for the life of me, I can't figure out who or why."

We asked about his new store, and Mr. Forster's face lit up. "If my wife and I didn't have that, I'm not sure we'd get through this. It's been our dream for a long time."

"When will it open?"

"We were set for this week, but that's not going to happen. And with people thinking I might be guilty of something, will anyone come?"

CHAPTER 26

☺ *Bryce* ☺

That night online so many people had so many different conversations going on that it was hard to get a word in. When someone mentioned Mr. Forster, I immediately typed in a response, but 20 or 30 messages had already posted on some other subject.

> BLT23: Hang on! Everybody stop for a minute and
> stick with one subject. The stuff you're writing
> about Mr. Forster isn't true. I talked with him this
> afternoon.
> Baileywickzzz: Where'd you see him, jail?
> Lollapawinner88: Of course Forster's going to say
> he isn't guilty. Everybody in jail is innocent, right?

> **Greenboy21:** Why don't you tell him to give
> **Ms. Prine's coins back?**
> **PingPongU:** Cut it out and let BLT23 have the floor.
> **What did Forster say?**

I didn't go into detail, but I briefly wrote what Mr. Forster had told us.

> **PingPongU:** Isn't there a possibility that all these peo-
> ple are right? that Forster is playing you?
> **BLT23:** Sure, I've thought of that, but I know the guy.
> He's not lying.

As I watched the other messages fly by, I thought about how powerful this tool was. More than 50 people were focused on all these messages. There was more energy here than in any class. If we could somehow harness this, we could use it for good—to help Mr. Forster instead of hurt him.

CHAPTER 27

✖ Ashley ✖

I showed the blue team pictures a missionary had given me, showing the poverty and starvation in an African village. The team voted to raise money to help the village get its own well and to provide seeds for planting.

At the same time, every member had found out about the Red Room and wanted to get in and spy on the other team. Hayley and others who knew Bryce's situation kept the pressure on me.

"It's not like you're doing anything wrong," Hayley had said. "It's just so we can keep an eye on them."

"I can't do that to my brother."

Duncan Swift had edged closer to me. "It would mean a lot to the team. It would build morale. Can you give it a shot?"

"Put yourself in my position," I said. "Suppose you had a twin and—"

"Look, if you're scared, I understand. . . ."

"I'm not scared. I just wouldn't want Bryce doing that to me."

"Yeah, 'do unto others' and all that stuff," Hayley said. "Blah, blah, blah. It means you don't care about us. We need to know their project so we can make ours better."

"I just don't think it's right."

I wrote all this in my diary that night while Bryce was downstairs typing away. My teammates had become distant, shunning me because of my decision.

I waited until I thought Bryce had come upstairs. Instead, it was Dylan walking to and from Mom and Sam's room, wearing the tightest pair of pajamas in history. He had one leg in his pajamas and was hopping from the stair railing to the wall and back again, trying to get his right foot in.

"Here, let me help you with that," I said.

I helped him pull them on, then tucked him into his car bed. He said thanks about a million times and asked if I'd read him a story.

"I think Mom wants you to go to sleep," I said.

"Just one!"

After I read him the shortest book I could find, I had to listen to what he wanted for breakfast, what he was going to do in kindergarten, his favorite color. . . .

I got him quiet enough that he grabbed his covers and stuck his thumb in his mouth, then pulled his door closed—leaving a small slit as requested—and headed back to my room. I passed Bryce's door and knocked. It opened a little, and I could tell he wasn't in there. I could hear him still tapping computer keys downstairs.

His jeans lay on the bed, and something purple stuck out of one pocket. I hadn't intended to snoop, but what could I do? I was curious. I slipped the paper out and saw something scrawled on it. Could it be the password for the chat room?

I stuffed the paper in my own pocket and hurried back to my room.

CHAPTER 28

☻ *Bryce* ☻

The next day I tried to explain my idea of helping Mr. Forster to Kael, but he didn't want to listen. Everyone I talked to had judged him. He was "guilty until proven innocent" in their minds, and I hoped I hadn't given away who I was in the chat room by telling them I talked to him personally.

In history class our teacher brought up the founding of America. Most of our teachers aren't *against* Christianity, but history is one place where God gets left out a lot. Listening to our teacher, you'd think God was on vacation at the founding of the country and hadn't been back since. Not once did our teacher mention that the people who came to America from England wanted religious freedom. Freedom to worship God.

From there it was on to the separation of church and state and how bad people were to bring religion and politics together. I just wanted to keep quiet, learn the dates and the people's names, names of the presidents, that kind of stuff, but I finally had to raise my hand.

"I thought that separation thing was to keep the government out of the church," I said, my voice shaky, "not to keep the church out of the government. What's wrong with people who are religious holding office? Some of our greatest presidents have asked God for help."

"Such as?" the teacher said.

"George Washington. He prayed at Valley Forge. And Abraham Lincoln believed God helped him become president so he could unite the country."

"There's no difference between that and the people who want to blow up America because they think God told them to," someone said behind me.

I looked back. Lynette.

"And what do you say to that, Bryce?" the teacher said.

My blood boiled. "I think it's crazy. To say that men who really wanted to do what God wanted them to do, to help people become free and be able to worship, are the same as terrorists who kill innocent people? When was the last time you heard about Christians as terrorists?"

"More evil has been done in the world because of religion," Lynette said, "more wars, more killings, than anything else."

I turned and faced her. "How many hospitals have atheists ever built? How many orphanages? How many homeless shelters are run by agnostics? Those places are started by people who believe every person is created by God and deserves to be cared for."

The room fell silent.

Sweat ran down my neck, my face felt hot, and my heart pounded like a hammer.

Lynette shook her head. "How many preachers run off with the church's money? And how many people kill because God told them to? The last school I went to, most kids were religious. They'd stand around the flagpole and sing songs and pray. Then I'd see those same kids cheat on tests and steal from the sandwich vendor outside the school. They'd make fun of my family and me because we don't believe like they do. Said we were going to hell."

She stared down at her desk, and I knew I had lost. You can shoot someone down with your words and win an argument but still lose. My goal wasn't to win but rather to help the others in class see the truth.

CHAPTER 29

❦ Ashley ❦

The purple paper burned a hole in my pocket, my brain, my heart. Part of me thought Bryce would never find out who had gotten the information. For that matter, I could slip the password into Hayley's student planner without her knowing who did it.

But I'll know.

The other person bothering me was Duncan. The closest he'd come to noticing me in the last two years was during tennis camp the past summer. And Hayley knew I had a crush on him. Was she using him to get information from me?

All through the morning I kept going back and forth, deciding to just give them the paper and instantly become everyone's favorite blue-team member, then crumpling it up and stuffing it deeper in my pocket. I couldn't bring myself to throw it away. When I'd think of Bryce and that I had taken it from his room, guilt would sweep over me. Then, when I thought how much my teammates would like me, I almost put Bryce out of my mind.

Jesus taught the golden rule—to treat other people the way you want to be treated. I wouldn't want Bryce giving my secrets away, but somehow this felt different.

Especially when I looked at Duncan. His hair was longer than the last time I'd seen him. It covered his forehead and just showed those deep blue eyes. When he looked at me during lunch, I tried to smile, then realized part of my peanut-butter-and-jelly sandwich was stuck to my teeth.

I was alone in Ms. Prine's class, waiting for the rest to come in, when I pulled out the wadded purple paper and spread it on my desk. If I could just throw it away or stick it over one of the Bunsen burners . . .

Hayley came up beside me. "Is that what I think it is?"

I nodded. "But I can't give it to you. It would be like—"

She ripped the page out of my hands and cackled. "Those people think they're so smart. This will help us more than you can imagine, Ashley. Thanks so much!"

I tried to grab the page back, but people started filing in, and Hayley stuffed it into her backpack.

"This is a big mistake," I said. "Let me have it back."

"Trust me," Hayley said. "It's not a mistake. You're going to be our team heroine."

In spite of myself, that almost sounded good.

CHAPTER 30

◔ *Bryce* ◔

Unfortunately, what most people wanted to talk about online that night was what happened in history.

> **Cabooseontheloose:** You should have heard Bryce. The veins were sticking out of his neck and everything. He sounded like a lawyer.
> **ChangesMade44:** Lynette made some good points, but Bryce owned her. If you're reading this, Lynette, don't feel bad. You'll get him next time.

I wanted to say something—anything—to clear my name. Even apologize for how strong I'd been. I held back, knowing everyone would know my screen name if I did.

But if I didn't say anything, people would realize that too. I didn't see PingPongU—the one I knew was Lynette—responding.

> **BLT23: Yeah, Bryce. I agree with what you said about God and all that, but you could have said it a lot nicer.**

I sat back and watched others react. Several chimed in and agreed, hopefully not knowing I had just written about myself.

Someone mentioned Mr. Forster and what a crook he was. I couldn't take it and jumped in with details of our discussion with him.

> **Schwinnsterama123: BLT, I can prove you're wrong about the whole Forster thing.**

Everyone fell strangely inactive. It was like this Schwinnsterama kid and I were the only two in the whole chat room.

> **BLT23: How?**
> **Schwinnsterama123: Walk three blocks north of where you met Forster and check out the new business. I'll bet someone has thrown something away that they shouldn't have.**
> **BLT23: How would you know?**
> **Schwinnsterama123: Just do it.**

CHAPTER 31

❀ Ashley ❀

I had my candle going and my diary in high gear, confessing all my sins, when Bryce burst into the room. He looked like he'd seen a ghost. I closed my diary faster than you can say, "Traitor!"

"We were being watched when we went to see Mr. Forster," he said. "Somebody online knew we were talking with him at the administration building. Have you told anybody?"

No, but I gave the whole blue team your password. I shook my head. "No, of course not."

"Then we were watched. Come on—we have to go to town."

"Now?" I said.

"I'll go by myself if you won't."

I grabbed my helmet and turned on the headset that let me talk with my brother while we rode. This would have been the perfect time to confess to him, but not through the headset. That didn't seem right.

"Three blocks north would put us at the old library, right?" I said.

"Exactly. But I can't imagine what we're supposed to find there."

It was still warm as the sun slipped behind the front range of mountains near our house. There was a certain smell to the air—football weather. Fall was approaching, and summer was putting on its coat and preparing to leave for seven or eight months. Where we live, summer lasts from about June until late August, but I've actually seen it snow in July. Flowers freeze here. You have to be really careful about what you plant.

We parked at Mrs. Watson's and walked to town. The shops and restaurants were bathed in the golden glow of the sun mixed with clouds. Lingering effects of a forest fire caused billowy clouds of smoke to cover part of the sky, like a gray scab over a blue wound.

Bryce stopped outside the old library. There were no lights on inside, but he knocked anyway. Three blocks back the administration building still looked like it was grinning at us.

We took a look around the front of the old library and peeked in the windows. Then we walked through the brick-lined alley toward the back. I wondered if people a hundred years ago had walked this same path, leafing through a Mark Twain or Charles Dickens book on their way home.

At the end of the alley sat a huge, green garbage bin. Empty paint cans were stacked beside it, along with lots of black garbage bags. Old boards, rotting ceiling tiles, and broken furniture stuck out of the bin. It looked like a demolition crew had gone wild.

Bryce went to the small porch that extended from the rear entrance. He rummaged through a pile of mildewed books and photos while I picked through the green bin.

"Maybe we'll find some old book worth a million, and we can give it to Mr. Forster," I said.

The garbage bags were all tied, and they gave me the creeps. I pictured mice or rats moving inside.

The alley was darker now, and as I stepped back, I thought I heard something move on the other side of the fence. A dog? A person?

If someone saw us at the administration building, maybe they're watching now. I glanced at the nearby houses and shops. Nothing.

I was about to walk back to Bryce when something in the bin caught my eye. Atop one of the tied garbage bags was something metal. Shiny. I moved closer.

"This is a wild-goose chase," Bryce said from the porch. "There's nothing here that—"

I held up a hand. "You'd better come here."

I pointed. On the garbage bag was a metal box that looked just like the one we'd seen the year before in Ms. Prine's cabinet. The lock had been pried off and the hinges bent.

Bryce reached for it but I stopped him. "Fingerprints."

He pulled out a tissue and picked up the box by the handle. It swung open and a piece of paper fell out.

I picked it up by one corner. A science test from last year with Ms. Prine's name on the top.

Other than that, the box was empty.

CHAPTER 32

☺ *Bryce* ☺

Finding the box in Mr. Forster's garbage sent my stomach to my knees, but it sure looked like he was being set up. Why would someone else know about this if they didn't plant it here?

I wrapped the box in newspaper and took it with us. I strapped it on the back of my four-wheeler, then stashed it inside the barn.

"How did the person who sent you the instant message know who you were?" Ashley said. "Aren't you supposed to be anonymous?"

"I've been the only one to stick up for Mr. Forster. When I talked about meeting him, he or she must have put it together."

I crawled in bed and stared out the window. A sliver of moonlight crossed my covers, and I wondered what to do. Who was Schwinnsterama123? Why did he/she spy on our meeting with Mr. Forster? How did he/she even know about it?

I couldn't sleep, so I slipped downstairs and logged on to the Red Room. No one was on. I called up the earlier conversation and re-read the interaction between Schwinnsterama123 and me.

Finally I typed, *Anybody here?*

I was about to shut the computer off when a message popped up.

> **Schwinnsterama123: What did you find?**
> **BLT23: You know.**
> **Schwinnsterama123: You told anyone?**
> **BLT23: Why do you want to hurt Mr. Forster? What are you hiding?**
> **Schwinnsterama123: HAVE YOU TOLD ANYONE?**
> **BLT23: What if I did? Did you set him up?**

The screen was blank for a few seconds. If I could get into this kid's head, maybe he would make a mistake and reveal himself.

> **Schwinnsterama123: You and your family won't be safe unless you turn that in to the police.**

CHAPTER 33

Ashley

Bryce acted edgy as we rode the bus to school, like Boo Heckler was going to jump out from under the seat. I asked him what was wrong, and he finally told me.

"Keep an eye out for who it might be," he said. "Watch your back."

I couldn't bring myself to tell Bryce that there were people from my team in that chat room and that it was my fault.

In first period, Boo Heckler sat yawning in his chair next to me. I tried to act like I was studying, but I could tell he was looking at me. I glanced up.

"Hey, how come you aren't riding your four-wheelers to school?"

"You noticed, huh?"

"They're nice machines."

"New rule, I guess."

"Bummer." He smiled and showed his little green teeth. "Want me to beat up the new principal?"

"I'm sure you could," I said, "but I don't think that's a good idea."

"I'd ride the things no matter what he said. What could he do? He can't tell you what you can do off school property."

I'd had the same thought, but the Bible talks about being obedient to those in authority, people like your parents, political leaders, and police. I assumed that included teachers and principals.

The first bell rang and as people filed in I said, "I'll bet you're pretty bummed yourself, not being able to go to high school."

He frowned. "My friends are all in ninth grade."

Boo has friends?

"I found out yesterday that that Forster guy had more to do with my flunking than I thought. A couple of teachers told me they pushed to let me graduate, but Forster made the decision. He's going to get what's coming to him."

CHAPTER 34

☺ *Bryce* ☺

I was studying every face. I was looking for yawns or red eyes, but that pretty much described the whole eighth grade.

I found Kael between classes, and he had a smile as wide as the Grand Canyon. "We're on to something with the Red Room, Timberline."

"How so?"

"Think what could happen if we market this around the country. Every middle school, high school, even elementary school would buy it. And my dad says if I come up with some software ideas, we could use the money for our project."

"The Red Room fund, huh?"

"Exactly. We could wind up like Bill Gates or some other billionaire. Make sure you're on tonight when we talk about our project."

"It'd be nice to talk about what we're supposed to when we're on there, Kael. Things could get out of hand if we're not careful."

"Stick with me, buddy. This is going to be the best idea any class *ever* had."

"Well, I need help. Do you know who Schwinnsterama123 is?"

"I couldn't tell you if I did. I don't know who any of the people are."

"Didn't you enter the names and passwords?"

"I gave that list to my dad—he helped me set the whole thing up and he tossed the list when he was done. You should probably just ask the person online, or go to the separate chat room. We put that up last night."

"Where's that?"

Kael explained how you could pair off with one or more people you'd agreed to talk with. I wrote the instructions in my notebook. I wondered if my stalker knew it was illegal to threaten someone over the Internet.

In gym class we had our choice of staying inside or doing the climbing wall outside. It was sunny, which describes just about every day in Colorado, and the wall didn't seem as crowded. Lynette was with the outside group, so I worked up the courage to talk with her. I hadn't spoken to her since our debate in history class.

Coach Baldwin strapped us into harnesses and let us go up two at a time. Most kids like to see how fast they can do it, but Coach Baldwin says you should climb like you have no bungee cords to simulate real mountain climbing.

I got in line behind Lynette on purpose. She had her hair up in a ponytail, and I could smell her perfume in the breeze that rushed past the building.

"This wall is new," I said. "Friend of mine is responsible for it."

She stared at me blankly. I wanted to say I knew she was PingPongU. She looked like she wanted to chew me out or hit me, but then her face softened. "I was so mad at you yesterday I could have spit."

"Sorry I came on so strong," I said. "And I'm sorry you've had a bad experience with church people."

"Never met anybody who's had a good experience."

"Timberline, you're up," Coach Baldwin said. "You too, Lynette."

We moved to the wall, got the harnesses attached to the bungee cords, and started the climb. From a distance, the outline of the climbing wall looks just like some of the red rocks our town is named after. As you move closer, you see the different colored foot- and handholds.

I showed Lynette some of the things my friend had put inside little chambers scattered through the climb: sports items, signed baseballs, basketballs, and pictures. She seemed touched by his story, and some of her anger seemed to wear off.

People yelled encouragement, partly because they wanted to see us reach the top—which not everybody does—and also, of course, because they wanted their turns.

At the top was a place to sit and look out at the school, the field, and in the distance, Pikes Peak. It just looked like a brown mound, and I told Lynette how it would probably snow up there before long. I pointed out a few of the mountains along the Front Range, and she asked where Cheyenne Mountain was, the home of NORAD.

She glanced at a plaque with a Bible verse on it, and I told her it meant a lot to me.

"All right, time to get down from there," Coach Baldwin yelled.

I turned to climb down and noticed someone with a hooded sweatshirt walking into the gymnasium. Weird, since the rest of us had shorts on. Whoever it was had something under his arm.

"Who's that?" I said to Lynette.

She turned and caught a glimpse of him as he walked through the door. "Nobody I know."

I told Coach Baldwin about him as soon as I reached the bottom. He quizzed me, then ran into the gym. The hooded sweatshirt guy was nowhere in sight.

"All right, everybody outside now!" Coach shouted.

CHAPTER 35

✖ Ashley ✖

We were in Ms. Prine's class working on a science crossword puzzle. For whatever reason, teachers give busywork the first week of school.

I was trying to figure out 15 across, a nine-letter word beginning with a *c*, meaning "a science dealing with properties of substances and their transformations," when the alarm rang. It wasn't the buzzer to change classes and was different than the fire alarm. It rang two seconds, stopped, rang another two seconds, and continued.

Ms. Prine's eyes bugged out, and she ran for the door and locked it.

I put my hands over my ears and hoped they'd shut the alarm off before we all went deaf.

As soon as the alarm stopped, Mr. Bookman's voice came over the speaker. "Students, stay in your classrooms. This is not a drill. We are on lockdown."

We looked at each other. It's times like this you wish Marion Quidley wasn't on the other team, because even if she didn't know what was going on, she'd have a theory.

A few minutes later emergency lights flashed outside, and a Red Rock police cruiser pulled up. Duncan whistled the theme to *The Andy Griffith Show*. The officers take their jobs seriously and are not anything like Barney Fife, but we all laughed as the guy got out of his car to Duncan's soundtrack.

Ms. Prine made him stop, and she watched the hallway closely.

You could hear the stress in Mr. Bookman's voice when he came back on the speaker. Mr. Forster had always tried to keep things calm and not get overexcited. "Teachers, keep your students in their rooms and away from the doors and windows. An intruder was sighted entering the gymnasium."

Bryce, I thought. *He's in gym right now.*

CHAPTER 36

☻ *Bryce* ☻

It was spooky huddling by the climbing wall outside the gym. There had been a few people inside who joined us. We all watched the closed doors, waiting for them to burst open and some crazed maniac to run out. My thoughts seemed to echo off the climbing wall behind us.

Coach Baldwin came back outside, but he wouldn't let us go to the locker room to get dressed or even get a drink. He said he wanted us where he could see us.

There are plenty of ways you can get out of the school, lots of doors and windows. But there are also lots of places to hide. The one that immediately came to mind was the subbasement boiler room. None of us were allowed down there alone, of course, but I'd seen it once when I'd helped Mr. Patterson move supplies. It would take the police the rest of the day to search the whole school.

The guys tried to act tough—me included—saying what we'd do if they caught the intruder, but the truth was we were as scared as the girls. It was at a Colorado high school north of us that two kids had taken guns to school and killed a bunch of students and teachers. It's happened at other schools several times since then, but that was the worst. People still talk about it.

Kael and others announced their theories about who the guy might be and what he wanted. Marion Quidley said she'd read a story that morning on the Internet about escaped convicts from Kansas thought to be on their way toward Colorado. That sent shivers down my spine, even if I wasn't sure I could believe her.

"Yeah, I'm sure the convicts traveled all the way from Kansas looking for our school," Carlos said. "Give me a break."

Marion muttered, "Jerk."

Carlos glared at her.

A police officer walked outside. I'd seen him a couple of times over the past few months, and when Coach Baldwin pointed at Lynette and me as the ones who had seen the intruder, he nodded at me.

We described the guy as best we could (though I said it could have been a female), and the officer took notes. "Did you get a look at the face?"

"It was covered by the hood," Lynette said.

"What about his clothes?"

"Jeans and a gray hooded sweatshirt," Lynette said.

I'd learned from reading and from my own investigations that being observant is really important. In Hardy Boys books (just like Nancy in Ashley's Nancy Drew books), Frank and Joe notice everything—shoe size, jewelry, scars, eye color, fingernail length. But I hadn't really been concentrating when we saw the guy. And we had been pretty far up. The only thing I could think of was that the sweatshirt had a blue ring around the middle.

The cop thanked us and headed for the locker rooms.

More sirens sounded as backup arrived. It was the most exciting thing to happen at the school since the snowstorm in the sixth grade when a bus went over a hill. Nobody was killed, but it was all we talked about for months.

After what seemed like a couple of hours, Mr. Bookman finally said the lockdown was over. "The building has been deemed clear. Thank you for your cooperation."

The way he said it made it sound like Lynette and I had made up the whole thing. I went to the locker room to change and reached in my gym bag. My hand banged something metal. I opened the bag wide for a better look.

Ms. Prine's metal box.

CHAPTER 37

❀ Ashley ❀

Bryce waved from the hallway before our next class, and Hayley giggled. I wanted to choke her. I had to do something to stop our team from spying on the Red Room.

Bryce was white as a sheet and carrying his gym bag. He unzipped it and held it up to me.

I thought there might be something crawling in there or a bloody sock or something even more gross. Bryce is not above pulling practical jokes. But he looked scared, so I looked in.

"Why did you bring that to school?"

"I didn't. After we saw the guy walk in the gym—"

"You're the one who saw him?"

"Me and a girl."

"You think the guy . . . ?" I paused to catch my breath. "What did you do with the box when we got home last night?"

"I put it in the barn—at the bottom of the stairs leading to Sam's office."

"That means someone went to our house," I said.

"He had to have been watching us—he knew where I put the box."

"But why? What does he want from us?"

Bryce pulled out his cell phone. "I'm calling home."

"You don't think he could have hurt Mom or Dylan, do you?"

"There's no answer."

"Call her cell," I said.

"Is there a reason you're not in class?" Mr. Bookman said.

"We're worried about our mom," I said.

Mr. Bookman stared at Bryce as he dialed.

Bryce shook his head. "No answer."

Mr. Bookman held out a hand. "I'll take that, Mr. Timberline." He snagged Bryce's cell phone. "These aren't allowed in school."

"But—"

"Refer to the student handbook."

"Can I get it back after school?"

"Sure. At the end of the year."

CHAPTER 38

☺ *Bryce* ☺

I stashed my gym bag in my locker and headed to class, making it just before the bell. Before my next class I raced to the pay phone outside the office and called home.

Still no answer.

I imagined Mom's hands bound with duct tape, Dylan locked in a closet, the hooded sweatshirt guy waiting for us.

The last hour dragged, and I watched the second hand tick like a snail crawling across a desert. I rushed to the office and called home again. Leigh answered.

"Is Mom there?" I said, out of breath.

"Haven't seen her."

"What about Dylan?"

"Bryce, I'm busy."

I pictured her putting cheese on her tortilla chips. "Look, this is important! Can you look around?"

"Oh, here she is," Leigh said.

"I've been out with Dylan," Mom said. "What's up?"

I said I'd tell her when I got home.

Ashley met me outside. My phone call made us miss our bus again. I had a feeling our visitor would show up via the Web that night.

Ashley stopped and turned back toward the school. "What's that all about?"

People stood near the climbing wall. The janitor had propped a ladder against it, and Mr. Bookman inched his way to the top a rung at a time.

"What's he doing?" Ashley said.

Lynette stood at the bottom of the ladder, watching, as Mr. Patterson held it steady.

CHAPTER 39

✖ Ashley ✖

The girl with the black hair was really cute, and I could tell Bryce felt uncomfortable around her. I hadn't seen her before.

We reached the ladder in time to hear Mr. Bookman give a loud "Hmm." He was staring at the plaque posted on top. I knew Mr. Bookman had no idea why that climbing wall was there or why there was a plaque with a Bible verse on it.

The verse read: "A friend is always loyal, and a brother is born to help in time of need." It was a tribute to Bryce after his friend Jeff's long battle with cancer. Most of the town had shown up at the dedication after the wall had been quietly installed.

"What's going on?" Bryce said.

Mr. Bookman dusted his hands, as if the ladder was the dirtiest thing he'd ever touched in his life. "We have a serious violation of church and state separation here. That plaque has to go."

"What?" Bryce yelled. He looked at the black-haired girl. "Did you have something to do with this?"

"I shouldn't have to look at that on school grounds. It offends me. I don't appreciate having religion shoved down my throat."

"It's not being shoved anywhere," Bryce said. "You had to climb all the way up there, and I had to point it out! The guy who had this built—"

"That's another problem," Mr. Bookman interrupted. "I can't find any permit to have this structure on school grounds."

"That's probably because the guy who—"

Mr. Bookman raised a hand. "Save the explanation. Mr. Patterson, arrange to have that removed immediately."

"I'll need to find the right tools," he said. "Those things are fastened by—"

"Then find them."

Bryce said he couldn't stand it and was going home. He gave Lynette a blank stare, and she returned it.

If they did take the plaque down, I wanted to be there to take it home or even give it to Jeff's parents. I never dreamed anyone would be upset by a quote from the Bible.

I moved next to the girl and said, "Hello, I'm Ashley, blue team."

She gave me a little smile and told me her name. She looked at Bryce walking across the field. "You know him?"

"Yeah," I said.

Lynette sighed. "He's on my team. Seems like a nice guy, but I think he's one of those Jesus freaks."

CHAPTER 40

☺ *Bryce* ☺

I ran through the fields toward our house. I'd lost my cell phone and had our barn invaded, and now my friend's plaque was being taken down. And how could the intruder have disappeared from the school?

What if it wasn't someone from outside the school? What if it was somebody pretending to come from the outside?

When I got inside I went straight to the computer and logged on to the Red Room. Kids were already talking about the event. Some thought Lynette and I had made up the story to get attention. I didn't see PingPongU.

Someone steered the conversation to our charitable idea. A few liked the idea of a sign for our middle school. The one we had was falling apart. On the first day back the sign had said, "Welcome Back Students!" The next day, after a strong wind, the sign read, "come Back dents!" as if a car insurance company had messed with the letters.

Another student suggested we raise money for cancer research and donate it in Jeff Alexander's name. Someone else said we should go together with the blue team so we could make the best use of our money, but that was quickly shot down. I guess the red team likes competition as much as the blue team.

To be honest, I didn't care what we raised money for. It all seemed so small after what had happened to Jeff, after what we'd been through in the Grand Canyon, after losing my dad. And if Mr. Forster could be railroaded out of the school by one of the students or . . .

Wait a minute, I thought. *What if this whole thing was concocted by one of the teachers? Or Mr. Bookman?*

A message popped up from Schwinnsterama123 asking if I was online. I thought about it for a minute, then typed back, *I'm here.*

Schwinnsterama123: Private chat. Now.

CHAPTER 41

❋ Ashley ❋

Mr. Patterson couldn't get the plaque off with his drill and told Mr. Bookman he'd finish in the morning. The principal didn't seem happy, but it was clear there was no way he was climbing up there and doing it himself.

Mr. Patterson had known Jeff, and I could tell he didn't want to take the plaque down. Maybe he thought the principal would change his mind overnight.

Ever since Hayley had gotten the password, I'd felt a distance between Bryce and me. That wasn't good, because if you had to pin me down about it, I'd say Bryce is my best friend.

At home I found Bryce at the computer and asked to talk.

"Can it wait?" he said. "I'm in the middle of something."

"I'd rather talk now. I have a confession."

He typed something on the computer and turned toward me.

They say confession is good for the soul, but until it's out, confession is murder on the stomach. Mine was doing flips, even though I knew it was the right thing to do.

Part of me wanted Bryce to think the whole thing was Hayley's fault, that she had taken the paper from me. But I had to remember where I got it in the first place, so just owning up to it would be better.

"So what's the confession?" Bryce said.

"I took something from your room, and I'm sorry."

"Took what?"

"A paper that was sticking out of your jeans pocket. I didn't know what it was at first, but then I figured it was the password to the Red Room."

"*You've* been spying on us?"

"No." I couldn't look at him. I bit my lip. I'd started the confession rolling, but now it felt like the thing weighed 500 pounds and I was pushing it uphill. "Someone at school took it from me. They actually asked me to get it from you."

I tried to explain the whole thing, but it came out jumbled, like a crumpled crossword puzzle. Bryce looked hurt, like I'd just cut the strings on his favorite tennis racket. The more I told him, the more slump-shouldered he became.

I was close to tears. "I'm really sorry, Bryce, and I don't blame you for hating me."

He closed his eyes. "I don't hate you, but I'm surprised. You could have just put the paper back in my pocket once you figured out what it was. Why'd you take it to school?"

That was a question my counselor, Mrs. Ogilvie, would ask. "I almost threw it away, but I guess I didn't like other people on the team looking down on me. In fact, I liked them thinking I had helped out."

"So they were more important than me?"

"No. I mean, it was partly because Duncan thought I might be able to get the password."

Bryce held up a hand. "Let's talk about this later."

He showed me the message from Schwinnsterama123 and said he was just about to have a private chat. "This could be the intruder at the school today."

"Bryce, what if this is a member of the blue team?"

"I can't remember if Schwinnsterama123 was online before you gave the password away." He set his jaw. "I'm ready to find out."

CHAPTER 42

☺ *Bryce* ☺

I wanted to be mad at Ashley, stalk off, slam a few doors, that kind of thing. At least give her the silent treatment for the rest of the night. But I had to chat with this Schwinnsterama character. I figured Ashley might help find out who it was, plus I might be able to use what she'd done to me later—you know, like to get her to do my chores.

I logged on to the private chat.

"Why'd you choose BLT23 for a screen name?" Ashley said.

I told her. "And I thought it was obscure enough that no one would figure it out."

"Guess it didn't work."

> Schwinnsterama123: Find my little present today?
> BLT23: People go to jail for breaking into homes.
> Schwinnsterama123: People who withhold evidence
> get in trouble too. Why didn't you take it to the po-
> lice?
> BLT23: Because I don't think Mr. Forster did any-
> thing.
> Schwinnsterama123: I can tell you right now—you're
> wrong. The guy's a crook. He cheats.
> BLT23: You knew the box was in the trash. Why
> didn't YOU tell the police?
> Schwinnsterama123: You and your sister are the hot
> detectives. They'd believe you.
> BLT23: What team are you on?
> Schwinnsterama123: What's important is that you
> turn that box in to the police and tell them where you
> found it.
> BLT23: Or what?
> Schwinnsterama123: I can make things very uncom-
> fortable for you and your sister.
> BLT23: You'd better hope the police can't trace you.
> Threats over the Internet are felonies.

"You really think this guy knows something about Mr. Forster?" Ashley said.

"I don't know, but we have to find out who he is."

CHAPTER 43

Ashley

The Red Room creeped me out so much that I didn't even want to go near the computer. It was like those animal magazines I used to have as a kid—I didn't like to even turn the pages of the ones that had pictures of snakes.

I closed my curtains because it felt like someone was watching me, though you can't really see many houses from our second floor.

It was even worse thinking that someone from the blue team might be the one threatening us, and I was responsible for that person getting the password.

I called Pippin into my room to sleep that night. Our other dog, Frodo, is not allowed upstairs because he tinkles on the bedspreads.

Pippin is a fluffy, white bichon frise and thinks he's one of us. He trotted in with a pair of Sam's white socks in his mouth (he stuffs them in the back of his kennel and sleeps on them), and it was funny to see his ears and those socks flopping around. Pippin hopped onto the bed, nosed his way under my covers, and put his head on the pillow next to mine.

Bryce came in. "What's going to happen to the plaque on the climbing wall?"

"I don't have a good feeling about it," I said. "Tell me about Lynette."

I read between the lines. He'd had some kind of tiff with her and felt bad about it. I've never seen Bryce in love before, so it was interesting.

I scooted close to Pippin and pulled the covers up. "Is there any part of you that thinks Mr. Forster is guilty of something?"

"Not unless we find those coins in his cash register." Bryce ran a hand through his hair. "I called Jeff's parents and told them there might be trouble with the climbing wall. Mr. Alexander sounded hurt."

"How do you feel about it?"

"Like if Mr. Forster were our principal, there wouldn't be a problem."

Bryce stared at my curtains, and I tried to think of something that would cheer him up. Pippin licked my hand.

"About the password . . . ," Bryce said.

I sat up. "Yeah?"

"I forgive you and everything, but it was a pretty rotten thing to do."

"I agree."

"I mean, if I'd have done that to you . . ."

"I probably would have screamed at you and hit you and run you around the backyard until your tongue plopped out."

He nodded. "Yeah, that sounds like a good punishment."

"I didn't have to tell you. I could have just kept it a secret."

"Yeah, and it would have eaten you alive. I'm glad you told me. Now we can gang up on Schwinnsterama."

"How?"

"I have an idea how we can out him."

"Or her," I said.

"It'll take both of us. You in?"

CHAPTER 44

☺ *Bryce* ☺

The next morning was overcast and foggy as the school bus wound around town. At school Ashley and I stopped in our tracks when we saw a white construction truck at the climbing wall. Someone was on top with tools, and it sounded like they were sawing the thing in half.

Mr. Patterson stood back from the group. He smiled at us as we walked up to him, then shook his head. "Sure is a shame. I tried to get it off without hurting it, but it was welded to a piece of metal."

"They're not going to take down the whole wall, are they?" I said.

"Don't think so, but Mr. Bookman said any display that even hints at religion has to be taken out. That's why they took away the football."

"The football? Why?"

"It was signed by a famous player and at the end he wrote, 'God bless.' Guess Mr. Bookman thinks that's going to corrupt the school-kids."

I shook my head. Sparks flew from a machine at the top of the wall. I was glad Jeff's parents weren't here to see it. It would have broken their hearts.

Other kids filed in from school buses, stopping to see what the fuss was about. A few late teachers walked across the parking lot. I noticed Harris, the silent kid from first period. He parked his bike at the steel rack.

A black car pulled into the parents' lot and circled in front of the gym entrance. The windows were tinted, and I could tell it was new to Colorado because the windshield didn't have dings in it. That and the Wyoming license plate gave it away.

Lynette stepped out, waved good-bye, then paused to look at the climbing wall.

"Happy now?" I yelled.

She glanced at me and headed inside.

CHAPTER 45

❃ Ashley ❃

I slipped into the science room before first period like Bryce and I had discussed. The cabinet door was open, and I inspected the lock. It didn't show any sign of forced entry, no marks outside or in. The front and sides of the cabinet were fine—Bryce thought perhaps someone had drilled a hole and filled it in.

I pulled a chair close and stood on it, scanning the top of the cabinet. Bryce's hunch was that whoever got to the coins didn't have a key. He wouldn't tell me why he thought that, but I felt so bad about what I'd done to him that he could have asked me to climb into some spider-infested back room and I'd have done it.

The top was fine, no drill marks, no holes. Just dust and a few books that looked like they needed cleaning.

There was only one thing left, and I couldn't do it alone. I looked for some strong guy. Only girls. I glanced at the clock—just a few minutes before class, and I had to get to Spanish. I remembered something Bryce had said to check for—scuff marks on the tile floor.

I knelt and held a tiny flashlight right in front of the cabinet. The floor looked shinier there, like someone had tried extra hard to clean it. But underneath the shine were marks, grooves in the tile. I switched to the other side, my heart beating faster. No scuff marks.

Boo Heckler ambled past the door, his big arms swinging.

"Aaron, can you give me a hand?" I said.

He started clapping, then laughed. "Was that enough of a hand for you?"

I laughed, pretending it was the funniest thing I'd ever heard. Four years ago maybe. Eighth grade, no way.

"I need you to pull this cabinet out a few inches," I said. "Can you?"

He spat on his hands and rubbed them together. *Lovely,* I thought. Then he grabbed the cabinet with both hands and lifted it off the ground. His face got red and he sputtered and coughed. But the cabinet moved a little, and in the same grooves on the floor.

"That enough?"

"Yeah, great. Stay here. I want you to move it back in a second."

He leaned against the chalkboard as I knelt behind the cabinet. There were wood shavings in the dust. I shone my flashlight along the back, and it didn't take long to find what I was looking for.

"What do you think you're doing?" someone said.

"Uh-oh," Boo said.

I turned. "Ms. Prine, I think I know how your coins were stolen."

CHAPTER 46

☺ *Bryce* ☺

What Ashley found made it unlikely that Mr. Forster had taken the coins. If he had the key, why break in?

I'd printed notes to Schwinnsterama123 on little slips of yellow paper and put them inside several lockers. I checked kids' last names first, but no one's last name started with *Sch.* I even checked the last names in our phone directory in case their parents were divorced and they had a different name. No luck.

The note read:

Schwinnsterama123,

Meet me at the flagpole during lunch. We need to work something out. I'm afraid of what might happen if we don't.
     BLT23

A few people with yellow strips tossed them in the hallway.

In science class Carlos came to me holding one. "Timberline, you get one of these?"

I took the strip, read it, and shook my head.

"Why would somebody put this in my locker? I'm not Schwinn-whatever."

I thought about going to the office and telling them that someone in the school had tried to hurt Mr. Forster. With Mr. Bookman in the front office, I wasn't going to take any chances. I trusted Mr. Gminski the most. He could be snarly, but I never questioned that he liked us and wanted the best for us.

Still, my gut told me to wait, not to talk to a teacher until I knew who Schwinnsterama123 was.

Before lunch I looked outside and saw that the white truck was gone from the climbing wall. The top of the wall was blocked by a tree, and I couldn't see the plaque. I hoped Mr. Bookman hadn't thrown it in the trash.

Lynette glanced at me as she walked to the back of the room. I hadn't given her a yellow strip because I knew her screen name. She held her books close to her chest and sat quickly. I wanted to tell her what a courageous person Jeff was, how he'd wanted to leave the climbing wall for people to enjoy, and that the plaque was his legacy. It was the most unselfish thing I'd ever seen.

Her complaint had caused the plaque to be removed. That made me angrier every time I thought of it.

CHAPTER 47

✖ Ashley ✖

I tried to talk with Hayley about the Red Room, but she cut me off. "It's been helpful to see what the red team's doing and how they're going to raise money. Who needs a stupid old sign out in front of the school? Anyway, we have you to thank."

"Don't thank me. It's wrong. We don't have to snoop on the other team to come up with a good idea."

She furrowed her brow and her face turned red. "Why are you so upset? It's not like we're trying to zap their invention. We're just peeking over their shoulder. Besides, all they have to do is change the password."

I'd have to tell Bryce to have Kael do that. "Has anyone from the blue team actually written something there, Hayley? We're looking for this Schwinnsterama123."

"Only a few of us have the password. That Schwinnster was there when I logged on the first time."

I turned to leave, but Hayley grabbed my arm. "You available for a meeting tonight?"

"Sure. What's up?"

"You haven't heard? We took our idea to the administration this morning. They shot it down."

"Why? What could be wrong with trying to help people dig a well and plant crops?"

"Mr. Bookman was all for it at first. He kept saying it would be good public relations for the school, until we told him it was your idea."

"Uh-oh."

"Yeah. He excused himself from the meeting, and I guess he looked up the sponsoring group on the Web site. Must have found something he didn't like."

"Separation of church and state," I muttered.

"What?"

"It's a Christian group that wants to help keep people from starving."

"Wish you'd have told us that at the start."

"It's not like they're making people sing a hymn in order to eat," I said.

"Still, it would've been nice to know. Now we're back to square one."

CHAPTER 48

☺ *Bryce* ☺

I stood near the flagpole feeling like a sitting duck with peanut butter breath, so I moved closer to the wall. From there I could watch anyone coming out of the cafeteria. I had passed out too many yellow slips, so any of the kids who got them could just watch and find out I was either Schwinn or BLT.

The climbing wall looked sad. I couldn't imagine what Jeff's parents would think if they saw it.

A couple of people stuck their heads out the door, then went back inside. I've always been an inside eater, preferring a table to the ground or the parking lot. Outside eaters aren't as popular. You'd never catch cheerleaders or anyone on the basketball team eating outside.

It didn't surprise me that Boo Heckler wandered outside alone. No lunch bag. I almost felt sorry for him. This was his fourth year in middle school, and there didn't seem to be a soul for him to talk to. He threw a rock into the parking lot. I waited for a windshield to shatter, but the rock bounced into the field.

When Boo noticed me I got that sick feeling, like I should have stayed inside. "Helped your sister out today. She tell you?"

"Yeah, thanks a lot."

We stood there awkwardly with nothing to say. In the past, Boo would have threatened me or just started pummeling me, but without his mean friends to encourage him, he seemed more—I don't know—human.

"Want half a sandwich?" I said.

"What kind?"

I told him.

He finally took it like a bear would snatch a baby salmon. He'd eaten the whole thing before I had a chance to take another bite of my half. I held out a bag of Fritos, and he scarfed them down like candy.

"Who you think took them coins?" Boo said, his mouth full.

People came out of the cafeteria, some throwing trash in a can near the flagpole.

"That's what we're trying to figure out," I said.

"Betcha it was Forster. Wish I could get my hands on him."

"Yeah, Ashley said you were ticked about what he did to you."

"Ruined my whole summer. Never got to see one ball game. Not even minor leagues."

"You like baseball?" I said.

"Yeah." He wadded the Frito bag and handed it to me like I was his personal waste-management employee. He leaned over and peeked inside my bag, and I pulled out a green apple. I wondered if this was like feeding squirrels—would he come back for more tomorrow?

"Why don't you ever eat lunch?" I said.

"I do," he said, crunching into the apple. "Sometimes I just forget to bring it."

I wondered about his parents. Had his mom stayed home with Boo or had she worked? What had made him such a bully?

I noticed something waving in the wind: a yellow piece of paper stuck to the flagpole.

"Excuse me," I said.

"You burp?"

I stopped and looked back. "No, just going over there."

I glanced at my watch as I moved toward the flagpole. Only a few minutes before next class. I tore the yellow paper from the pole.

> *BLT23,*
> *I have nothing to say to you. Leave me alone.*
> *Schwinnsterama123*

CHAPTER 49

❀ Ashley ❀

The meeting that night was at the Toot Toot Café. The owners, a kind old couple named Crumpus, let us put a couple of tables together. The Toot Toot serves the best meat loaf in town and has the thickest milk shakes west of the Mississippi.

All the girls except me said they weren't really hungry, that they couldn't eat a thing. I thought that was because guys were there, so I was ready to order a whole basket of French fries and a huge mocha milk shake, just to prove my independence.

That's when Duncan Swift walked in. He moved like an ice

skater, always in control. His hair sparkled and swished against his neck.

"What can I get you, Ashley?" Mrs. Crumpus said.

"Water is fine," I said.

The guys ordered onion rings, buffalo wings, extra large milk shakes, and cheeseburgers. It was like watching pigs pull up to the trough. I wanted to cast demons from them and send them to the parking lot, if you know what I mean.

Hayley called the meeting to order (over the crunching and slurping) and said we needed to come up with a new project.

"What was wrong with the well in Africa?" Duncan said. "That was cool."

Hayley explained, and everybody looked at me. My face felt hot, and I tried to cool it off with a long drink.

"Has the red team decided what they're going to do?" Chuck Burly said. Vegetable oil dripped from his fingers.

We went back and forth about whether to use information gleaned from the other team's Web site. Duncan said there were plenty of people on our team who could write a computer program to raise money, but I said that would be cheating.

"It's the American way," Duncan said. "Competition."

"Doesn't matter anyway," Hayley said. "They already changed the password. We can't look at the Red Room anymore unless we get the new one."

"Don't look at me," I said. "Let's just come up with something even more creative than them."

"How about a new plaque for the climbing wall?" someone said.

"A helicopter," someone else said.

"New sod for the football field."

"New socks for Coach Baldwin."

We finally agreed that the biggest need at the school was a new sign after all. Hayley offered to find out how much it would cost—though she still thought it was a dumb idea—and the rest of us were supposed to come up with more moneymaking ideas.

I couldn't help thinking of Ms. Prine's coins. I wondered if they were worth as much as a new school sign.

CHAPTER 50

☻ *Bryce* ☻

The Red Room felt dead that night, though a lot of people weighed in on different subjects. I watched for Schwinnsterama123 and even asked for him a couple of times. Had I scared him away? He was the one trying to intimidate Ashley and me with the stolen box. Had he lost his nerve?

There's something about the end of the first full week of school. By then you know each class, each teacher, what's expected of you, how much homework you'll have every day, and whether the classes are going to be much fun. I was ready for the week to be over so I could go to the video store and choose a good action movie or video game and just veg.

Mr. Gminski gave me work I figured would take about two weeks—filing all the old forensics-meet scores that had been thrown into about 10 cardboard boxes.

"Why do you keep this stuff?"

"Because when you become a hot movie star, I'll be able to dig in here, get your evaluation sheet, sell it on eBay, and retire."

I almost believed him.

Before I could move to the first box, the school secretary beeped the intercom and called me to the office.

"What'd you do now?" Mr. Gminski said with a smirk.

The secretary motioned to Principal Bookman's office with her eyes. I walked in, and he asked me to close the door. Behind the door was another ominous sign: the plaque from the top of the climbing wall. I figured the meeting might be about that. Instead, Mr. Bookman pulled out the yellow sheet of paper I had written to lure Schwinnsterama123 into the open.

"Did you write that?" he said.

I thought about calling a lawyer or pleading the Fifth Amendment—refusing to answer on the grounds that I might incriminate myself. "Yes," I said. "Who gave it to you?"

He pursed his lips. "What is important is that you realize how serious this is."

"Mr. Bookman, you don't understand. I—"

"Mr. Timberline, the student who gave me this has asked that we go to the authorities. He wants a restraining order against you."

He, I thought. *So it* is *a he.* "What's a restraining order?"

"A legal document prohibiting you from coming within a certain distance of the other person. It's so you won't further threaten or menace that person."

"How can I be ordered to keep away from someone I don't even know? Who is this guy?"

"Is it true you met in a chat room? One that keeps you both anonymous?"

"Yes, and *he's* the one who's been threatening *me*, not the other way around."

"I've talked with . . . the other party, and he's willing to give you another chance. Don't attempt to make contact and everything will be fine. Understand?"

I stared at the floor, trying to make sense of everything.

"Mr. Timberline, if there's a restraining order, we'll need to get your parents down here and—"

"Okay, I understand."

"Good," Mr. Bookman said.

I stopped at the secretary's desk on my way out. "Did another eighth grader meet with Mr. Bookman this morning?"

She smiled. "I'm sorry. I can't say."

CHAPTER 51

❀ Ashley ❀

Bryce and I spent Saturday at an alpaca farm helping the Morris family. Mr. Morris offered to pay us, but it was enough to be in the open pasture with Buck, the family's Great Pyrenees, and our alpaca, Amazing Grace. Mr. Morris had given her to us a few months earlier.

The Morrises have three boys who bounce around the farm like miniature Tiggers, and they're fun to watch. In the evening, Mom, Sam, and Dylan joined us for a cookout. Bryce went inside now and then to watch some baseball game, but I liked sitting outside waiting for the stars. Of course they're always there—we just can't see them.

On our way home, Bryce asked if he and I could go to a different church in the morning.

"What's wrong with our church?" Mom said.

"Nothing," he said. "We just want to try the one that meets at our school."

Sam gave us a look in the rearview mirror like that answer didn't compute.

"Actually, we just want to ride our ATVs again," I said.

"Want to come with us, Sam?" Bryce said.

Sam isn't a Christian and usually goes to church with Mom only on Christmas and Easter or when Bryce and I are in some kind of program.

Sam smiled in the rearview mirror again. That didn't compute either. No way was he coming with us.

CHAPTER 52

◔ *Bryce* ◔

Too bad Ashley and I could ride our ATVs only on Sunday. We looked weird wearing our Sunday clothes and helmets. As it turned out, the other people at church all wore jeans and T-shirts, so we were two of the best dressed there.

Signs at both sides of the school read The Flock. I knew why they might call it that, but I wasn't sure what people passing would think. The Bible compares followers of God to sheep. They're kind of dumb animals that have to have a shepherd, which is where God comes in. But The Flock made it sound like the middle school had been turned into a barn. Maybe on their new property they'd have one, complete with bales of hay.

"Feel guilty about going to church to investigate?" Ashley said.

I shrugged. "I'm still going to sing and listen."

The room was set up like I'd never seen it. Onstage stood a full band plus several singers at microphones. Banners with biblical phrases and attributes of God hung from the ceiling. Lights focused on a cross. A huge screen displayed a colorful picture of Pikes Peak. The image had been altered to include green grass and a big field of flowers in the foreground.

Ashley raised her eyebrows as we found a place to sit. A man smiled at us and gave us each a bulletin. It had a list of songs, a list of pastors, a list of meetings, and a list of people who needed prayer. There were Bible studies for overweight people, gamblers, alcoholics, shopaholics, grief recovery (including for pet loss), and a whole page of other classes.

"There sure seems to be a lot going on here," Ashley said.

Their music was a lot different from our church. I soon realized they were singing the same worship songs we sing, but I'd never heard them like this.

When the pastor got up to preach, you'd have thought he was just a regular guy from the congregation giving announcements. He told a funny story about how hard it was for his family to make it to church without fighting. Then he opened the Bible and taught about taming the tongue.

I looked around and saw a few people from the red team.

The Sunday school classes had been held before the worship service, so as soon as the pastor said a final prayer, people filed out the side door or to the nurseries.

I grabbed Ashley's arm. "Let's go."

❋ Ashley ❋

I hate when Bryce grabs my arm, especially when I see somebody I want to talk to, but I waved, mouthed *I'm sorry,* and followed
him. Soon I was back in familiar territory. The office was straight
ahead, and I wondered what Mr. Bookman would say about these
services. He'd shut down this church faster than me driving an ATV
in the hallways with a Frappuccino.

We walked through a maze of parents picking up their kids. The
infant nursery was in the upstairs library. This looked like a church
with a lot of young families.

We moved to the science room, and I noticed one of Dylan's

friends from preschool. He was decked out in the latest cartoon craze. His shirt, pants, and little hat matched, and he even wore light-up shoes.

Someone had put temporary latches on all the drawers and doors. These people sure did a lot of work every Sunday to get the place ready.

There were two adult workers and two young volunteers. I recognized one from band—Elaine Zimmel.

"I didn't know you guys went here," she said, her braces glinting.

"Just visiting," I said.

"Anybody else from school volunteer here?" Bryce said.

"Yeah, we sign up for three weeks at a time."

"Who was in here last month?" he said.

She opened a red three-ring binder, unsnapped a laminated sheet, and handed it to Bryce. I read over his shoulder but didn't recognize any names.

Bryce bit his cheek. "Anybody else who might have been in here, other than you guys?"

Elaine shrugged.

Someone turned the corner at the end of the hall, stood by the lockers, and stared right at us.

I punched Bryce on the shoulder, but as soon as Bryce turned, the guy was gone.

CHAPTER 54

○ *Bryce* ○

I didn't see his face, but the guy looked about the same height as the person with the hooded sweatshirt. Ashley and I raced down the long hallway and turned the corner.

Nothing.

We got to the end of the next set of lockers and looked both ways. The hallways circled and intersected, and it could get really confusing if you didn't know your way around.

"You go that way and—"

A metal door clanged, and we both took off toward the sound. If it led outside, we probably wouldn't catch the guy.

Ashley turned the corner first and gasped. "The boiler room."

I kept going, hit the door, and almost fell down a flight of steps. They were metal, the kind with holes in them, and you could see into the storage area. Portable green boards, used sports equipment, mops, buckets, and more lay below.

I let the door close behind us, and the room went dark. I fumbled for a light switch. We were losing time, so I told Ashley just to hold the door open, and I hurried down, my shoes clanging.

I turned the corner and found a maze of pipes and wires. I know what a water heater looks like, but I'd never seen one this big. In fact, there were three down here and enough cobwebs to cover Red Rock 10 times over.

I let my eyes get accustomed to the dimly lit room, looking everywhere for movement. It seemed things were getting darker when someone came up behind me. I turned, ready to fight. It was Ashley.

"Don't do that!" I said.

"I'm not leaving you here alone," she said. "I propped the door open."

"I don't know where else to look."

"I do," Ashley said, pointing to the subbasement door.

CHAPTER 55

✖ Ashley ✖

I'd never been to the subbasement, let alone the boiler room, and the idea sent shivers down my spine. Plus the cobwebs were getting in my hair. Bryce seemed to enjoy the spooky room.

We moved slowly to the door, watching, watching. I spotted something red on a metal shelf.

"Flashlight," I said.

He clicked it on, and the beam hit two beady eyes that scurried under the shelves.

"Just a mouse," Bryce said.

I didn't care. I hate mice.

Bryce opened the door and pointed the light down another set of metal stairs. Why couldn't the people we chase run to a tree house or even a Dairy Queen? Why'd they always have to run for the spookiest, most desolate spot?

"Coming?" Bryce said.

I followed a step behind.

"We know you're down here!" Bryce yelled, and I almost jumped out of my skin.

We were down the steps and about to the middle of the room when I heard something behind us.

"Up there!" I shouted, turning to the door.

Bryce swung his flashlight around, but not fast enough. The door closed with a bang, and the lock clicked.

"We're trapped," he said.

CHAPTER 56

◉ *Bryce* ◉

I guess this was why they didn't want kids in the subbasement. I banged on the door, and when I put my ear to the cold metal I heard the boiler-room door slam above us.

I gave Ashley the flashlight, thinking that might calm her. She shook so hard that the light flickered against the far wall like one of those old silent movies. The light hit another pair of eyes, and it didn't look like a mouse's. More like a cat with a long, thin tail. Probably a rat.

"We have to get out of here!" Ashley said.

"Calm down. We will."

"When?"

"What day is it?" I said.

"This is not funny, Bryce!"

"You should have stayed up there and held the door, but you had to follow me."

"You think I wanted to come down here? I was trying to help." She banged on the door and screamed.

I grabbed the flashlight and walked through the room. I found a huge pipe I thought led to the sewer. I've seen movies where people crawl through things like this to escape, but there was no way we could have opened that pipe.

I found a toolbox and chose a pipe wrench and hammer. I handed the hammer to Ashley. "Try this."

She banged on the door with all her might, and the sound was deafening. Still, I didn't think anybody would hear us unless they came into the boiler room. I took the wrench and found the big sewer pipe. It was a long shot, but someone might hear the banging through the pipe. I used the Morse code sign for help, rapping out SOS as three dots, three dashes, and three dots, but finally gave up and just banged away.

I pushed the light on my watch. It had been 20 minutes since church had ended, and if everybody was like my family, they were headed home. I hoped the people in charge of takedown were still here.

Ashley sank to the top stair but kept pounding with her fist. I dropped the wrench and joined her.

"It's not like we're going to run out of air down here," I said. "We can't die that way."

"Real comforting, Bryce."

"Eventually Mom and Sam will come looking for us, see our ATVs in the parking lot—"

"And what? Break into the school? Nobody in their right mind would think we're down here. Why would they?"

I slid and backed my seat up to the door and bounced my head against it.

Think.

CHAPTER 57

❀ Ashley ❀

When you're locked in a dark room with no hope of anyone finding you, and the flashlight starts flickering like a spent candle, you begin to understand why a person would start losing it.

That person was me.

I imagined someone finding Bryce and me 100 years from now, our bones at the top of the stairs, linked in a final hug. Mice building nests in my shoes. I'm telling you, I was getting pretty far out there.

Bryce kept looking at his watch. I think he was just as scared as I was, but he tried not to show it. When he took the flashlight I tried to grab it, and he nearly fell down the stairs.

"Keep pounding," he said. "I've got an idea."

I smacked the hammer against the door like Paul Bunyan chopping a metal tree. The noise was getting to me—my head ached and my stomach growled from hunger. (I imagined dinner on the table at home—all my favorite foods.) What if I broke off the door handle? Would we suddenly be free?

Clink, clink went the handle. That reminded me of a children's book my dad used to read us, and just thinking of him brought tears to my eyes. But I couldn't give in to the emotion. I had to keep trying.

The knob didn't break off, but I sure put some serious dents in it. It was no use. Whoever had locked us in used a dead bolt, and I didn't like the sound of that word. Bryce was in the corner, but his light had grown so dim I couldn't make out what he was doing.

Something metal creaked, and the light went out. Smacking sounds, and the flashlight came on again. Then a huge *snap!*

"What did you do?" I said.

He hurried back to the stairs. "If there're still people here, that might bring them. Keep pounding."

As we hit the door, Bryce explained that he had found the main circuit breaker for the whole building and turned it off. If he was right, all the electricity in the building was out. "If anybody's still around, they'll have to come down here to fix it."

"Yeah, if anybody's still here."

CHAPTER 58

☺ *Bryce* ☺

It was cool in the subbasement, but all the banging and yelling helped keep our blood going.

I remembered a news story about a pizza delivery guy who went on a run and didn't return. His boss couldn't reach him and his family worried. Four days later they found him stuck in an elevator, alive.

The flashlight was dead now, and I could tell from Ashley's breathing that she was desperate. We'd been locked in here less than a half hour, but it felt like 20 years on a deserted island.

For the first time, I thought to pray. I'm not proud of it, but it's the truth. We'd just spent more than an hour singing about God's wonderful love, how much he cares for us, and hearing a sermon about God listening in on all our conversations, and we hadn't even turned to the one who had control over such things.

I stopped banging and leaned against the door. I felt strange praying out loud, but Ashley's seen me at my worst.

"God, we really need your help right now. Please send someone to find us. And help us not panic. Jesus, I know you understand how scared we are. Please help us get out of here."

CHAPTER 59

❀ Ashley ❀

Bryce's voice calmed me. I'd prayed silently, but they were more like "arrow" prayers. You know, "Help, God," which was like saying, "Oops, get us out of this."

Stuff happens for a reason. Maybe God wants to teach you something. Maybe he allows something like your father dying in a plane crash. No matter what, God can use that in your life. I'm not saying it's easy, but it's what I believe.

Suddenly I got my mind off how scared I was and onto what God was trying to teach us. Or show us. The truth was that Bryce and I had come upon someone who either didn't like us or was at least mixed up in this whole mystery.

"Father, thanks for taking care of us. You've helped us so many times. I know you love us and want the best for us. There's nothing that can separate us from your love, not even a stinky, dark basement or somebody who wants to lock us in. So thanks for watching out for us, and please help us get out of here and get to the bottom of what's going on."

There's a story in the New Testament about two guys, Paul and Silas, who sit in a jail praying and singing all night. I figured Bryce and I could do that if we tried. At least it would have made me forget how hungry I was.

As it turned out, we didn't need to sing. We heard the sweet sound of keys jangling and footsteps down the steel staircase. Bryce and I hit the door again, banging away and screaming at the top of our lungs.

The dead bolt clicked and the door swung open. A flashlight shone in our faces, and I shielded my eyes.

"What in the world are you two doing down here?"

CHAPTER 60

◍ *Bryce* ◍

I recognized Mr. Patterson's voice immediately. He swung the flashlight away from our faces, and I saw his look of concern. He looked at the other side of the door with all the dents and the mangled knob.

"Sorry," Ashley said. "We were scared."

"I'll bet you were," Mr. Patterson said. "What happened?"

I told him as he walked down to the circuit breaker. When he'd flipped the lever, we hurried up the stairs. All our fears melted when we saw the sunlight. His was the only car in the parking lot. Our ATVs sat where we'd parked them.

"Somebody locked you in there by accident?" he said, squinting at the sun.

"We were following a suspect," I said. "You're not going to tell Mr. Bookman, are you?"

He scratched his stubbly chin. "I don't know that I have to, but I'm worried that somebody wanted to hurt you two."

"How did you find us?" Ashley said.

"I make sure the building is secure after the church service," he said. "And sometimes I move the lunch tables so I don't have to do it in the morning."

"So you heard us?" I said.

"I took a quick look around, locked the front door, and headed for my car. There's a ball game on this afternoon, and I wanted to see it."

"What made you come back?" Ashley said.

I was sure God had answered our prayers and sent an angel to tap him on the shoulder. Or maybe Mr. Patterson was putting his key in the ignition when he got a feeling that something wasn't right and he just had to go back inside.

Mr. Patterson shoved his hands in his pockets and looked at his feet. "I had to go to the bathroom."

I'll take it, I thought. *God can use even that.*

"I was in there when the lights went out," he continued. "I could tell the lights were on down the street, so it had to be the school's electrical system. That sent me down there."

I asked Mr. Patterson if there was any other way out, and he mentioned the air ducts and how we could remove a panel. I was glad we didn't have to crawl through those dusty things.

CHAPTER 61

❀ Ashley ❀

We were late for lunch, and it was sub sandwiches instead of all my favorites, but it was the best meal I'd ever had. Bryce and I wolfed our food.

"Service must have run late," Mom said.

Bryce and I looked at each other, our mouths full. As soon as we were finished we moved outside, where Leigh was washing her car. Pippin and Frodo licked at the water hose.

"Churches usually have a directory, right?" I said.

Bryce nodded. "Why?"

"We match people who attend with people in school."

I called Elaine, my friend in the nursery, and she said we could borrow her directory. "How'd you like our church?"

"Great," I said. "Worship was awesome."

An hour later we were poring over the directory. I called out a last name, and Bryce looked for a match in the yearbook. When we'd gone through the whole thing, we had a dozen names, but none seemed to fit the profile of Schwinnsterama.

"What if this doesn't have anything to do with a person at the church?" I said. "Somebody could have come in off the street and stolen those coins."

"And just happened to be there when we showed up today?" Bryce sighed. "Something ties a person on this list with Mr. Forster, but what?"

Bryce logged on to the Red Room, looking at me when he typed in the new password. We watched for a few minutes. Then he asked for Schwinnsterama123, but there was no response.

"You think Mr. Forster would be able to put things together for us?" Bryce said.

I shrugged. "Let's look for him at his new store."

CHAPTER 62

☺ *Bryce* ☺

The sky turned light blue, and there was plenty of daylight left. It was the time of year when summer doesn't want to give up, but you can feel fall shoving it out of the way. One day the temperature soared into the 80s, and the next it would struggle to break 70.

We parked our ATVs at Mrs. Watson's and headed into town. A couple of high school football players sat outside the Toot Toot Café, their feet hanging over the edge of rocking chairs. They were sucking down milk shakes and enjoying their day of freedom from practice, I guess.

Ashley noticed a light inside Mr. Forster's new business, so we cupped our hands around our faces and looked in the front window. Mrs. Forster was there. We'd never talked to her other than to say hello at a band concert or basketball game. She was short, not much taller than Ashley, and thin. Her blonde hair was cut like some European fashion model's—sticking out all over like it had a mind of its own. Her face also looked like a model's—sculpted nose, perfect teeth. When she saw us she smiled, but I couldn't help but detect sadness too.

She unlocked the door. "You're from the school, aren't you?"

Ashley introduced us and Mrs. Forster said, "Of course. Tom has told me so much about you. Come in."

The Forsters were nowhere near ready to open. Bookshelves were clean but empty. Juice machines sat in boxes on a dusty counter.

"Tom isn't here," Mrs. Forster said. "His brother's passing through Denver and had a couple hours' layover. They're having dinner."

She pulled out three stools and we sat.

"Does Mr. Forster miss school?" I said.

She smiled wearily and nodded. "He'd have gone crazy without this store to look forward to. He hates sitting behind a desk. He loves people. I think he even loves all the problems with students and their parents."

"So working at the administration building is killing him."

"I've seen his light fade. Whoever accused him did a good job." Mrs. Forster moved boxes and drew circles in the dust. "We wanted children. That was our dream when we moved here, to start a family. I'd stay home. But it hasn't worked out."

"I don't mean to be rude," Ashley said, "but since you mentioned it, can't you have kids?"

"The doctor says it's unlikely. We've talked about adopting. . . ."

It was as if a cloud had moved over her. Her face fell, and she didn't look like some European model anymore. "I'm sorry. I should get back to work."

"Need any help?" Ashley said.

CHAPTER 63

❋ Ashley ❋

We dusted, moved boxes, even shelved three boxes of books before the sun started to fade. Mrs. Forster's story made me sad. Some parents have children who make big mistakes, get in trouble, and mess up their lives. But it must be even worse to not be able to have your own child.

Mrs. Forster gave us their new phone number, which they got after receiving some weird calls. She also said they would know Mr. Forster's fate Thursday when the school board met.

As we walked back to our ATVs, Bryce said, "We have to solve this before then."

I took out our list of names. "Anybody live close to here?"

"Harris rides a bike to school." Bryce pointed at his address. "Isn't that street behind Mrs. Watson's house?"

We cut through Mrs. Watson's backyard and climbed a fence that kept her dog, Peanuts, from roaming the neighborhood. A small housing development called Grassy Knolls lay just behind a field. The houses had been built in the last few years and were all close together. Backyard fences surrounded swing sets and sandboxes.

We took the long way around and hit a cul-de-sac, where kids had dragged a basketball hoop. We had the address—123 Chisolm Lane—but we weren't sure where the street was. Bryce asked some kids if they knew where Harris lived, and they looked at us like we were celebrities. Anybody above fifth grade is considered in another universe.

A short kid with a big head pointed. "Two blocks over, middle of the street."

CHAPTER 64

☺ *Bryce* ☺

The front yards were mostly concrete driveways and sidewalks. Harris's house looked like the others, just a slightly different color. The garage door was open, and there was an empty space for a car, along with a motorcycle and a bicycle inside.

I rang the doorbell. Through the small window at the side of the door I saw movement. The church directory said Harris had an older brother, Terrill. On the wall across from the door were family pictures. I recognized Harris's picture—same as the one in our yearbook. His brother was to his left, and there was an older photo of the whole family in the middle. Next to the pictures was a shelf with model bicycles on it, like the one in the garage.

The door opened slightly. "Help you?"

"Harris? Is that you?"

He stepped out. "Timberline? I thought . . ."

"You thought what?" I said.

He glanced at Ashley, then back at me like he was watching a tennis ball fly back and forth across the net.

"We visited your church today," I said. "Were you there?"

"I-I don't want to talk to you."

"Why? What's wrong?"

"Bookman said he'd talk to you."

On the banister behind him hung a gray hooded sweatshirt.

"Mr. Bookman? I don't underst—"

Harris slammed the door.

Ashley looked as mystified as me.

We slowly moved away from the door. I stopped at the garage and stared at the bicycle. It looked 100 years old, though it had been freshly painted.

My mouth dropped open.

"What is it?" Ashley said.

"I think I just figured it out."

We took off down the driveway. I looked back and noticed someone staring at us from an upstairs window.

CHAPTER 65

❀ Ashley ❀

Bryce and I ran all the way to our ATVs and put on our helmets, activating our headsets as we started the machines.

"That bike of his is a classic Schwinn in perfect condition."

I gasped. "Harris is Schwinnster?"

"That's why he knew Mr. Bookman had talked to me. He must be the one who wants the restraining order against me. Kael said he started the Red Room to help people speak their minds when they wouldn't feel free to otherwise. He doesn't know how right he was."

"Harris stole the coins? locked us in the basement? was the one in the sweatshirt and has something against Mr. Forster?"

"He doesn't seem the type, but appearances can be deceiving."

"Bryce, he was scared out of his mind when he saw you. What could he have against Mr. Forster?"

I had a sick feeling about school from the moment I awoke the next morning. All the clues pointed to Harris, but we had no hard evidence. Bryce couldn't find the Red Room threats on our computer. I couldn't believe Harris had locked us in the basement or made life miserable for Mr. Forster or come to our house. I'd never been on his team and didn't know him. I had to change that.

Bryce was still upstairs getting ready when Leigh bounded down.

"Can I get a ride to school?" I said.

"Sorry, I'm late."

"Can you just drop me off at the turn? I'll walk the rest of the way."

"Sorry," she said as she grabbed her books and spun out the door.

Stepsisters, I thought.

I had to get to school fast so I could catch Harris. I couldn't wait for the bus, and even if I ran I'd probably be late. Then I saw the Ashleymobile, my ATV. I had to get to school.

I gunned the engine across the field and prayed I wouldn't be too late (and that Mr. Bookman wouldn't be outside watching). I made it to Mrs. Watson's in record time and hurried to the school entrance. A couple of buses were already there and kids filed inside. I waved at Hayley, who was laughing and talking with Duncan Swift.

This day was starting really badly.

Soon I noticed Harris's bicycle coming through the parking lot. Bryce was right—the thing looked like a classic I'd seen in movies about kids in the 1950s. He had to really be into bikes to ride something like that, because other kids probably teased him.

Harris parked and chained his bike. He unzipped his backpack and pulled out a stack of papers. When he saw me coming he nearly dropped them. He headed toward the entrance.

"Harris," I said. "I want to talk."

"I don't," he said, walking past me.

"I don't think it was you," I said.

That stopped him. He turned slowly and pushed his glasses back on his nose. "Me? I didn't do anything wrong. Your brother threatened me."

"Threatened you? Bryce never—"

"I have it right here," he said. "All the things he wrote. The list of students he said he'd hurt. I'm showing it to the principal right now."

CHAPTER 66

◔ *Bryce* ◔

I couldn't believe it when Mom said Ashley had left without me. She wasn't at the bus stop, and we didn't pass her on the way to school. I spotted her ATV at Mrs. Watson's. What was Ashley thinking?

I was headed to first period when Ashley caught up with me. Before she could tell me what was going on, Mr. Bookman said, "Timberline, in the office—now."

The secretary, who had always seemed polite, looked at me like I had stepped on her cat. In Mr. Bookman's office I found Harris in one of the overstuffed chairs. In front of him lay a stack of papers.

"New information has come to light," Mr. Bookman said.

"Honestly, sir," I said, "I didn't know he was the one—"

"Were you at his home yesterday?"

"Yeah, my sister and I—"

"So you admit you've harassed him."

"Harassed? No, it's the other way around. He's the one who—"

"Don't lie, Timberline," Harris said, suddenly not so shy and reserved. He held up the papers. "I have it in black and white—the stuff you wrote me, the people you were going to hurt, including Mr. Bookman."

I stood. "What? I never said anything like that."

He shoved the papers into my hands.

"Sit down, Mr. Timberline," Mr. Bookman said.

CHAPTER 67

✖ Ashley ✖

I prayed like crazy for Bryce as I went to first period. I couldn't concentrate on anything except what might be happening in Mr. Bookman's office.

"Hey, Ashley," Chuck Burly said in the hall. "What's going on with Bryce? He in trouble?"

"I'm not sure."

Rumors spread through the class. Boo Heckler wasn't in Spanish, and someone said he and Bryce had been in a fight. When Boo shuffled in late, the rumors switched to Bryce's ATV. Then to the stolen coins.

Before Mrs. Sanchez came in, Mr. Patterson stuck his head in the door. "How you doing this morning, Miss Timberline?"

I stepped into the hall. "Bryce is in trouble. They're accusing him of stuff he never did, and I don't know what to do."

"You want me to tell what happened yesterday?" he said.

"Please," I said.

He patted me on the shoulder. "I'll see what I can do."

I got a sick feeling. What if Mr. Patterson was involved? What if he had locked us downstairs? Could he have a problem with Mr. Forster? It didn't make sense, since he was the one who freed us, and he seemed like such a sweet man. The whole thing just confused me.

CHAPTER 68

☺ *Bryce* ☺

I think I can tell when people are lying. Their body language changes, they won't look at you, or they get nervous. I didn't sense any of that with Harris. He was angry, looked me straight in the eye, and pushed the papers in front of me without hesitation.

"I told my brother what was going on," Harris said. "When he saw the stuff BLT23 was writing, he suggested I print it for evidence."

"Is that your name when you're in this Red Room?" Mr. Bookman said.

"Yeah. And you're Schwinnsterama123, right, Harris?"

"Right."

"How did you know who I was?" I said.

"I suspected the first night when you said 'we.' I figured you were talking about you and your sister. But I wasn't sure until you grabbed my message from the flagpole."

"And you saw my sister and me at the trash can behind Mr. Forster's shop."

Harris squinted at me like I had 12 heads. "I don't know what you're talking about."

"The coin box you stole, the one that showed up in my gym bag the day we had the intruder."

"You have the coins?" Mr. Bookman said.

"No. Harris wrote me that I'd find something in the trash behind Mr. Forster's new store."

"That's a lie. I never wrote anything like that."

"Do you have any proof, Mr. Timberline?"

"No. The computer erased it."

"Right," Harris said.

When I finally looked at Harris's printouts, I couldn't believe it.

Schwinnsterama, if I catch you on that girlie bike of yours, you won't make it home in one piece. Your parents will have to scrape you off the sidewalk.

You're toast, Harris. And if you go to Bookman with any of this, you won't like what happens.

"This is crazy," I said. "I didn't write any of this. I didn't even know it was you until yesterday."

"You're denying you wrote this?" Mr. Bookman said.

"I swear, this is the first time I've ever seen any of it. Ask anybody who knows me. I would never threaten one of my classmates."

There was a knock on the door. Mr. Bookman went to answer it.

I turned to Harris. "Were you at church yesterday?"

"Yeah, why?"

"My sister and I were there. We've been trying to figure out who has it in for Mr. Forster, and we think it might be someone who attends."

"It's not me."

"Well, someone locked my sister and me in the subbasement. We came to your house last night because you're one of the school families listed in the directory."

Harris looked away. "Leave me alone."

Mr. Bookman returned. "You were at the school yesterday? locked in the basement?"

I nodded. "By someone who doesn't want us snooping around this case."

"Case?" Mr. Bookman said, clearly fighting a smile. I was insulted. "This *case,* as you call it, is easily solved. Just admit what you've done."

"I've done nothing," I said, my voice suddenly shaky. I hate it when I sound guilty, especially when I'm not. But being accused can do that to a person. I leafed through Harris's papers and found a page filled with curse words. And something was weird about the pages. Every capital *R* had a little hole in the curved part of the letter.

> *I'm going to run you over with my three-wheeler and smash you into the dust!*

First, of course, I don't swear. And I don't ride a three-wheeler either. My mind reeled. Was Harris the culprit? Why would he want to hurt Mr. Forster? Whoever wrote this knew Harris and me and our screen names.

Mr. Bookman moved to the phone. "I need your confession, Bryce, or I'm calling the police."

CHAPTER 69

❀ Ashley ❀

It was my longest morning ever. Between classes I went to the office, but the door was still closed. Mr. Patterson sat near the secretary's desk with a troubled look.

I was worried sick by lunchtime and sat eating a sandwich in almost the exact spot where I'd been singing 24 hours earlier. I was relieved when Bryce showed up, but he looked like he'd been through the spin cycle of our washing machine. He dropped his lunch beside me and left it unopened.

"What?" I said. "Tell me."

He told me everything. I couldn't believe what he said was on those pages or that anyone could think my brother would use that language. "So, did Bookman call the police?"

"No. He called Kael in and got his dad on the phone. The Red Room is closed permanently. Then he said he's going to bring in Mom and Sam and Harris's parents for a conference."

"What about the restraining order?"

"He threatened to tell the police, but I don't think he really wants to risk ruining his reputation as a strong leader. I promised I wouldn't even breathe in Harris's direction."

"Mom and Sam are going to be upset."

"They ought to be! *I'm* upset. This is not how I planned to start eighth grade. I just can't figure out where this is coming from if Harris is telling the truth."

I whispered, "What about Mr. Patterson?"

Bryce shook his head. "He busted us out of the basement. And he stuck up for me. Stayed in the office until I got out of there."

"Then it *has* to be Harris. He could have faked those pages, right?"

"Ash, you should have seen his face. He was scared of me. I mean, terrified I was going to hurt him. And how could he have gone to our house, brought the box to school, and gotten out of class to come in the gym?"

"Maybe he's working with someone else," I said.

CHAPTER 70

◔ *Bryce* ◔

Mr. Bookman had told Mom and Sam not only about me, but also about Ashley riding her ATV. Sam took the keys to both machines until they sorted things out.

"Ashley was just trying to help," I said.

When I told them the whole story, including the box being taken from our barn, Mom put a hand over her mouth. "Someone was at our house?"

Sam sat in front of the fireplace, leaning forward, elbows on knees. "Why didn't you tell us what happened after church yesterday?"

"We didn't want to worry you. Plus, we thought we had the thing figured out . . . until this morning."

Mom sighed. "I've tried hard to be here for you. To listen to your problems. If you don't trust me enough to—"

Sam shook his head and Mom sat back. I'd seen them like this in conversations with Leigh—shouting matches actually. It hurt to think I'd hurt them, especially unintentionally.

"They want us to bring the computer in," Sam said. "If there's anything on there . . ."

"Take it," I said. "It'll prove I'm telling the truth."

"We're on your team," Sam said in his growly voice, "and we believe you."

Something as big as a baseball seemed to grow in my chest, and my eyes stung. Sam's support took a huge load off me. I wondered what my real dad would have said, and I knew it would have been similar.

"We can solve this," I said. "We're close. Real close."

Sam nodded. "Just be careful." He stood and took Mom's hand. "Your mother and I have to pay a little visit to your new principal. He sounds wrapped pretty tight."

CHAPTER 71

❀ Ashley ❀

I called members of the blue team who had known the password, but all of them denied writing anything—they said they just watched.

"Our biggest suspect is Harris," Bryce said. "If he's the intruder, he's also the one who locked us in the basement."

"But why would he do that?"

"To scare us," he said. "He made up the chat-room stuff to get us to stop our investigation. He doesn't want us to figure this out."

"How does it link with Mr. Forster?"

Bryce pulled Mr. Forster's phone number from his wallet and

dialed, turning on the speakerphone. "Is there anyone at the church who didn't like you?"

"They spilled coffee a couple of times and we had to have the carpet cleaned, but it was no big deal," Mr. Forster said.

Bryce asked about Harris, but Mr. Forster said he'd never had any problems with him.

"What about Mr. Patterson?" Bryce said.

Mr. Forster chuckled. "He's probably the most gentle man I've ever known. Wouldn't hurt a fly, let alone get me kicked out of school."

Kicked out of school, I thought. It sounded funny coming from our ex-principal.

Bryce asked about teachers, students, coaches, even coaches from opposing teams.

Mr. Forster said he could think of no one.

"How about people in town who don't want you to start your business?" Bryce said.

"The owner at Johnny's Pawn and Deli wasn't happy at first, since we're selling old books. But when I told him how many sandwiches we'd probably order, he welcomed us." Mr. Forster sounded tired. "I'm really sorry this has happened to you and your sister."

When Bryce hung up he ran a hand through his hair. "We can't talk with Harris, Mr. Forster has no clues, and I'm the suspect."

CHAPTER 72

☺ *Bryce* ☺

If the first day of school is all excitement, the second week is dullness squared. The reality of the year sets in, and people get sick or come in late. Usually, driving our ATVs wakes me up, the brisk wind whipping at my face, but since Ashley and I had to walk or ride the bus, I yawned the whole way.

Sometimes the best thing you can do about a problem is not think about it. Do something else to take your mind off it. But the night before, I'd dreamed of Harris locking our whole family in a bank vault. Inside was a computer that spit printouts of bad e-mails.

The only good thing that had come out of Mom and Sam finding out about our problem was that Sam got my cell phone back from Mr. Bookman. No way was I going to lose it again.

I saw Marion Quidley in a seat near the back of the bus and sat behind her. Usually I want to stay as far away from her as I can, because she kind of likes me. But I also knew Harris didn't have many friends, and I'd seen him and Marion talking.

"Heard you were kicked out of school," Marion said.

It made me wonder where she got her information and whether I could trust anything she said about Harris. I asked what she could tell me about him, whether they were friends, and if anything was different this year as opposed to last.

"Just family stuff," Marion said. "His mother remarried a couple of years ago, and Harris took the new guy's name. I think he goes to a shrink and I've seen him take medicine, so I figure the doctor prescribed something."

"When I talked with him the other day," I said, "it felt like two different people: the kid I see in class and the one in the office."

Marion nodded. "He's usually quiet and reserved, but I've seen him intense. Like Jekyll and Hyde." She turned around. "A religious person like yourself probably doesn't believe in split personalities— you probably think there's some kind of spiritual problem."

"I don't know what to think," I said.

CHAPTER 73

✖ Ashley ✖

At the last stop, Bryce slipped into the seat behind me. He looked like he'd seen a ghost. He kept whispering, and I asked him to talk louder.

"Another theory," he said. "We've counted Harris out because he's a nice guy and acted like he was really scared."

"New information?"

"What if the e-mails written to Harris were actually written by his other personality?"

"Now you're freaking me out," I said. It sounded like one of those

Frank Peretti books with the bad angels fighting good angels and people caught in between.

"If there really is something wrong with Harris, he could write the stuff to himself and not even know it. Like one part of him has turned into Boo Heckler, and the other part is still Harris. I know it sounds creepy, and it's a long shot, but—"

"How could we find out?" I said. "We can't even talk to him."

"His doctor?"

"They keep all that stuff confidential."

"School nurse?"

"Same thing."

Bryce leaned forward until his head rested on the back of my seat. He snapped his fingers. "I got it."

The kid in front of us, a sixth grader, looked back like he was scared.

I nodded toward Bryce and said, "He's not feeling well."

"Leigh," Bryce said. "If she can find the older brother, she can ask him what's going on. She ought to be able to find out something."

"Only one problem," I said. "How do we get Leigh to do anything for us?"

"You have any money?"

"Spent it all on extra school stuff," I said.

Bryce winced. "I'm tapped too. But you'll think of something, right?"

As soon as we were inside the school, I went to the pay phone and used my last quarters to call Leigh's cell phone. She sounded annoyed that I'd called her and even more annoyed when I told her what I wanted.

"I don't get into your little mysteries," she said.

With the promise that Bryce and I would wash her car twice each week for a whole month, she said she'd *try* to find Harris's brother and *try* to talk with him, but that I had to agree to the washings even if she never talked with the guy.

I told Leigh she should be a lawyer, but I agreed to her conditions.

CHAPTER 74

☺ *Bryce* ☺

Mr. Gminski was in a bad mood, and I could tell the pixies didn't know how to handle it. He told me to take the roll and then left.

After I finished I told the kids that he could be like a cornered bear if he hadn't had his coffee. "If he yells at you, don't take it personally. He's just caffeine challenged."

When he returned with a Styrofoam cup and a smile, the kids stifled giggles.

I found the stack of boxes to file and was glad to be doing something mindless. Or so I thought. Each piece of paper told a story about someone. I put aside one evaluation form for a name that looked familiar. Mr. Gminski said the guy was now playing in the NBA.

"No wonder you want to keep these," I said.

I wondered how Mr. Gminski had collected all of them, but looking at his office and all the trinkets and photos let me know. He couldn't throw away anything. He probably still had all his baby teeth at home.

I pulled a picture out of one stack and was surprised to see Mr. Gminski, Mr. Forster, and other teachers. Behind them were kids with medals and trophies. Everybody was smiling except for one guy with no medal around his neck. I thought I recognized him but couldn't place him.

"You didn't know Mr. Forster was into forensics?" Mr. Gminski said. "He was amazing at oral interp in college. Actually got a partial scholarship from a small school in Indiana."

"Was he a judge?" I said.

"Exactly. If you find some of his forms, you'll see how thorough he was. He'd spend so much time writing his evaluation that kids and parents complained. He really enjoyed it."

"He hasn't been a judge since I've been here. Is there a reason?"

Mr. Gminski shrugged. "He asked me to find someone else. Simple as that."

"Why?"

"Maybe he wanted to spend more time with his wife. It's been so long I can't remember."

CHAPTER 75

❀ Ashley ❀

Bryce said he was going to walk into town. I rode the bus home and saw Leigh as we pulled up to the bus stop. She had a green water hose and a bucket beside her car. "Millie's getting a little dirty. Don't use the harsh detergent."

"Millie?" I said.

"It's better than the Ashleymobile. Now be careful with this spot here—the paint is kind of peeling."

"Did you find out anything?"

"About what?" she said. Then she smiled. Leigh watched as I sprayed the front grill. "Well, it took me a while to find Terrill.

Randy said one of the guys on his baseball team knew him, so I asked—"

"Can we get to the good stuff?" I said.

She sighed. "Make sure you get those bugs on the windshield. Anyway, I finally found him in an English classroom practicing some speech. Didn't seem like a speech kind of guy, but I hear he's pretty good. When he came out I acted like I was all impressed and asked if he'd had lunch. He said he didn't eat lunch."

Leigh was usually tight-lipped about everything, but now she was spewing information like a hose.

"So I put on the charm and walked with him to the commons, just talking. I told him my dad had gotten remarried and that set him off. He started ripping on his stepdad and saying his little brother was taking it extra hard—hey, watch that water!"

"Sorry," I said.

"So I asked him what this was doing to his little brother. He said Harris is being bullied at his school and is seeing a psychiatrist and taking medicine and the whole shooting match.

"Here's the good part," Leigh said. "I asked what happens if his brother doesn't take his medicine, and Terrill says he goes crazy. He seems like another person, kind of like you when you don't take your meds."

I looked up and just happened to lift the water hose again.

Leigh screamed something about not telling me anything else if I did that one more time.

CHAPTER 76

☙ *Bryce* ☙

I stopped at Johnny's Pawn and Deli and talked to the owner. He had tattoos, and his hair was tied in a ponytail with rubber bands. I asked if anyone had tried to sell him old coins lately. I described them and he said, "Those sound like the ones stolen from the middle school. Police asked me about them last week. Nothing so far."

I thanked him and moved to the administration building, where I found Mr. Forster in his office. Papers were strewn across his desk, and I remembered his wife saying how much he loved people.

"I was wondering about your forensics-tournament experience," I said. "Mr. Gminski told me you used to be pretty good."

His face lit up. "Those were some great days. I remember one story I read in high school. Two gang leaders get trapped, and instead of killing each other, they work out their differences. But before they can tell their gangs they don't need to fight anymore, they're both killed."

"Sounds scary."

He closed his eyes and recited a couple of sentences from the story, after all those years.

"So you were a logical choice for a judge," I said.

"I loved it because I'd had some pretty rough judges when I was young. I tried to be constructive in all my critiques, though I could be hard when I needed to be."

I pulled out the picture I'd found and showed it to him.

Mr. Forster shook his head. "Look at that tie. And how much hair I've lost."

"You remember this meet?"

He nodded. "Tight competition. Lots of emotion. The kids really wanted to win and yelled when they found out their scores. Some cried. It was pretty charged."

"Was anybody mad at you?"

He shrugged. "I don't remember. Why?"

I pointed out the somber guy. "Remember him?"

Mr. Forster took off his glasses and looked closer. "I think he was one I judged, but I don't recall—"

His phone rang and he answered. He covered the mouthpiece and said, "I need to take this."

I nodded and headed home.

CHAPTER 77

❋ Ashley ❋

I gave Bryce the news from Leigh, and he told me about his trip to town. We both thought we should tell someone about Harris's situation. He might be the culprit.

"Who do we talk to?" I said.

"Maybe Mr. Gminski?"

While I wrote a letter outlining what we'd discovered, Bryce searched for the forensics coach at a school in Colorado Springs. The guy with the long face in the picture was wearing the insignia of that school.

He clicked on the school's Web site and found a name. Cross-referencing the name with an Internet search, he came up with a phone number.

I was finishing the letter when Bryce snapped his fingers for a pen and wrote something.

"Hang on—do you mind if I put you on speakerphone?" he said. He punched the button, and I heard the scratchy voice of an older woman.

"Terry was so upset after that meet. He thought he should have won, but because one judge gave him bad marks he got second place."

"And he was in oral interp?" Bryce said.

"That's right."

"Do you remember the judge?"

"My memory is pretty good, but I don't think I can remember that. I do recall it was a man, I think from Red Rock. . . ."

Bryce looked at me. "It wouldn't have been a Mr. Forster, would it?"

"Actually I think it was. Now how did you know that?"

CHAPTER 78

☻ *Bryce* ☻

I kept my distance from Harris the next day, though I did watch him at lunch. He didn't sit with anybody, and he kept looking over his shoulder.

After school, Ashley tagged along to the offices of the *Red Rock Post.* She didn't have a clue what I was looking for, and I didn't tell her in case I was wrong.

We passed Mr. Forster's new store, which looked good enough to open, but it was still closed. My heart skipped a beat when I thought we were close to having Mr. Forster back.

You get a certain feeling when you've figured out a mystery, the pieces falling into place like some life-size jigsaw puzzle. I hoped this would be the last clue we'd need.

I asked for Mrs. Jensen, who I'd talked with during lunch. She was the editorial writer, the features writer, and sometimes the sportswriter. She even delivered the papers to the local grocery stores.

"You wanted to see the letter to the editor from Mr. Forster," she said, pulling out a large file and plopping it onto the wooden desktop. "We save these for a month. Looks like we need to toss a few."

She found the letter, turned the page around, and pushed it toward me. My hands were shaking.

"What are we looking for?" Ashley said.

"The letterhead is from the middle school," I said. "But of course many people would have access to that."

"Even someone from the church," she said.

"Right. But look at this. Every capital R has a flaw, which has been colored in."

I turned the page over and held it up to the light. Little black dots spotted the page where the writer had filled in those flaws.

Mrs. Jensen watched with a hand on her hip. "What's all that mean?"

"It means we now know who really wrote this," I said, "and why."

CHAPTER 79

❋ Ashley ❋

We cut through Mrs. Watson's yard and into the subdivision where Harris lived. We sat on the curb down the street and watched his house.

Bryce called the church office. We were sure we'd figured out the mystery. No doubt the letter to the editor and the e-mails had been printed by the same machine, and that machine was in Harris's house. After talking with the church secretary, we had placed the suspect at the church on the day we'd been locked in the basement. The only thing we weren't sure of was where the stolen coins were.

"It's going to take more than just accusing him and hoping he confesses," Bryce said. "He's probably thought of a hundred answers to anything we might bring up. The key is to catch him off guard."

"How?"

Bryce scratched his chin. "We need to somehow make sure he's at the school-board meeting tomorrow."

CHAPTER 80

◔ *Bryce* ◔

Mr. Bookman looked skeptical, but when I told him I thought my idea would lure the real culprit into the open, he seemed intrigued. However, when I told him I couldn't give him all the information, he shut down and wouldn't listen.

"There's no way I can take this to the superintendent," he said.

"Then I'll talk with him."

As I headed out of the office, Mr. and Mrs. Alexander—my friend Jeff's parents—stepped inside. I could tell it was hard for them to be in Jeff's school.

"This is really something, isn't it?" Mr. Alexander said.

"Yeah," I said, "separation of church and state gone wild."

They were in Mr. Bookman's office only a few minutes. When they came out, Mrs. Alexander was wiping her eyes. Mr. Alexander carried the plaque with the verse on it.

"Feel free to visit any time you like," Mr. Bookman called after them, as if nothing was wrong, as if nothing had happened.

CHAPTER 81

Ashley

For a mere one added month of car washings (and dryings), Bryce and I got Leigh to phone our suspect and tell him about the school-board hearing for Mr. Forster.

Next we met Superintendent Mauban in the parking lot and asked if he thought we'd be able to present information at the hearing.

"We don't discriminate," he said. "Young and old are free to participate."

As we made our way back home, we saw Lynette going into the library.

"Don't you think you two should settle things?" I said. "You know it's going to bother you if you don't talk with her. You can't leave something like this alone."

"What do I say?"

"Just tell her how you feel."

"Easy for you to say," he muttered.

CHAPTER 82

☻ *Bryce* ☻

Lynette was going through the stacks in the fiction section, so I milled around until she noticed me.

"Oh, hi," I said. "Fancy meeting you here."

"I do my homework here," she said.

"I'm sorry," I said. "I don't mean to bother you, but I have to tell you something."

I knelt beside the small table as Lynette sat. "I wanted to make sure we were okay. You know, about all the stuff going on. I apologize for what I've said. I hope we can be friends."

She stared at me, then got a far-off look in her eyes. "Wow. Some speech."

"I meant it."

She opened her notebook and smoothed out the page. "Next you'll tell me you're praying for my soul and that you want me to sing 'Kumbaya' with you at the flagpole. If it makes you feel better, go ahead and apologize." Her voice got louder. "I'm *not* sorry about our disagreement. I'm right and you're wrong. You want to believe in your religious fairy tales and base your life on a lie and make yourself feel better by making everybody like you."

I was so stunned that I stood, my knees popping, and walked out.

"How'd it go?" Ashley said.

"Fine. Good idea to have a chat."

CHAPTER 83

❈ Ashley ❈

It wasn't until we were walking across town after school the next day that Bryce told me what had happened in the library.

The meeting at the school administration building had started when we got there. A long table stretched across the front of the room, and all the board members had microphones. Dr. Mauban sat in the middle, reading with his glasses way down on his nose. Padded chairs filled the room, but only the first five rows were full.

Mr. Forster and his wife sat in the front row.

"Is our suspect here, Bryce?" I whispered.

He shook his head.

"What do we do if he doesn't show up?" I said.

"He won't be able to stay away."

Dr. Mauban recognized several kids for their excellence on tests. There was a report on the CATs and where the district fell in the results. Then came the financial reports—diesel fuel for buses, a property issue, and voting for the purchase of a trailer for the high school.

I was nodding off when the superintendent moved to personnel issues, or as he called it, "Human Resources."

Bryce looked behind us. "Still not here."

CHAPTER 84

☾ *Bryce* ☾

Dr. Mauban read the accusations against Mr. Forster: several anonymous complaints ranging from his being a threat to students to stealing money from the school. Dr. Mauban said they had investigated the embezzlement charges and there was no money missing. The letter to the editor in the local paper showed "reckless disregard," though Dr. Mauban noted that the letter was in dispute. There was a legal question about whether a structure built on school property violated the separation of church and state. And finally, there was the suspicion of Mr. Forster related to the stolen coins.

"Tom has been a valued member of the team here," Dr. Mauban

said, taking off his glasses, "and I've watched him grow. But I have to admit these charges demanded further attention, and that's why we put him on administrative leave. Tom, would you like to respond?"

Just then Mr. Bookman walked in and sat in the last row. I elbowed Ashley.

Mr. Forster stood at a microphone. "I want to thank the board for giving me this opportunity." His voice was thin and higher pitched than usual. "I was a troublemaker as a kid. Spent more time in the office than the principal, I think. But my third-grade teacher let me help her after school, let me take attendance and do other chores. One day she made an offhand comment about my being a leader and what a good teacher I'd make. I can point to that day, that second, and tell you that's when I became a teacher. I've never really wanted to be anything else.

"The past couple of weeks, including missing the first day of school, have shown me how much I love working with people, *for* people. Every one of these allegations against me is false. I would never write a letter like that to my closest friend, let alone send it to a newspaper. I don't know anything about Ms. Prine's missing coins—that I can assure you.

"As for the climbing wall memorial, maybe I should have run that through different channels, but my heart went out to that young man and I said yes. I take full responsibility for that action."

From the looks on the faces of the board, I didn't like his chances.

As Mr. Forster sat, I noticed a window at the back and a small room that looked like it was used to record the meetings. The lights were out overhead, but the glow of the equipment cast an eerie light on the face of the guy running the machine. Behind him someone in a white shirt moved.

Dr. Mauban asked if anyone would like to speak on Mr. Forster's behalf, and several lined up at the microphone.

"Stand in line, Ash," I said. "I'll be right back."

I slipped out the back and found the recording room. It was dark and it took a few seconds for my eyes to adjust. I finally saw the guy in the white shirt lean forward and say something. My heart raced.

I headed back and stood in line behind Ashley. "Suspect is here," I said, "but we need help."

CHAPTER 85

✖ Ashley ✖

I ran out of the administration building and looked both ways. No adults. No strong guy who could stand guard.

God, I need your help to find someone. Please.

Children's squeals rang from a nearby playground. Little kids played basketball at an eight-foot-high basket. On the other end, teenagers played slam dunk with their shirts off.

Standing at the edge of the building and smoking was Boo Heckler.

"Is this your answer, God?" I whispered.

When Boo saw me he put his cigarette behind him, as if I was going to tell on him. "What are you doing here, Timberline?"

"I need help, Fernando."

CHAPTER 86

☺ *Bryce* ☺

The longer I waited, the more nervous I got. I was relieved when Ashley came back. "Find anybody?" I said.

"I had to tell him there might be a reward, but yeah."

Finally, it was my turn. I pulled the microphone down and it squealed. "Sorry."

"Go ahead," Dr. Mauban said.

"When my sister and I moved here after our dad died, Mr. Forster was nice to us."

Mr. Bookman sat with his arms folded.

"He really seems to care about the person and not just how we do on tests and stuff.

"When I heard he wasn't back this fall, I was really bummed. Then I heard some of the reasons, and my sister and I started looking into it. One of the things against him is this letter to the editor."

I held up the page and showed them the weird *R*s. "We've found the printer that was used to print this, and it wasn't at the school. In fact, it was used to print some mean messages I was falsely accused of sending."

The crowd tittered and people whispered.

Dr. Mauban cleared his throat. "May I see those pages?"

I handed them to him and went back to the microphone. "My sister and I thought from the start that the things Mr. Forster was being accused of just didn't fit. Then Ms. Prine's coins turned up missing, and we found that the back had been taken off her cabinet.

"The more we looked, the more trouble we found, so we figured somebody might be mad at Mr. Forster. And we think we know who it is."

Even the board members with their Palm Pilots looked up at me.

"He's back in that room," I said, pointing.

Everyone stood and looked. The door opened and someone rushed out, but a few seconds later, Boo Heckler dragged Harris's older brother, Terry, into the room. Boo looked proud of himself.

"Let go of me!" Terry shouted.

Dr. Mauban strode back and escorted Terry to the front. He was red in the face and his hair hung in his eyes.

"I think this was the reason he was angry," I said, holding up the evaluation sheet.

Mr. Forster read it. "Is what Bryce says true, Terry?"

"I should have been first!" Terry yelled. "You took it from me. You don't know how much I wanted to hurt you for that."

Mr. Forster looked straight at him. "I remember your performance. You needed work on your delivery, but you were good. There's nothing wrong with second place."

"Maybe not for you," Terry said through gritted teeth.

It was painful, but when Dr. Mauban asked if Terry had done all these things to get back at Mr. Forster, he confessed. He gave Ashley and me a steely-eyed look. "I've got the coins at home. I was going to give them back."

CHAPTER 87

✖ Ashley ✖

"I found out about the Red Room thing and pretended I was a student," Terry said. "Sometimes Harris was on. Other times, it was me. Later I sent bogus threats to Harris. That's how he got all those."

"So Mr. Timberline had nothing to do with those messages?"

"No, that was me."

"What about the coins?" Dr. Mauban said.

"Harris had told me about them. I was on the cleaning crew one Sunday and pried the back off the cabinet before the service. When I found out the Timberlines were looking into this, I put the box behind the new juice place. I was going to plant the coins inside the business, but I couldn't get in."

I wanted to ask him how he found the box in our barn, but he was in enough trouble.

"That's a long time to hold a grudge, son," Dr. Mauban said.

Terry looked at Mr. Forster. "I promised myself I'd get you somehow. When my family moved here, I wanted to see you suffer."

Mr. Forster nodded. "It almost worked." He knelt in front of Terry, and everybody else moved back. "I'm sorry my telling the truth caused you pain. I hope you're still performing."

"I'm still trying."

"Good."

Boo Heckler tapped me on the shoulder. "You didn't tell me I was helping Forster. So where's my reward?"

CHAPTER 88

☺ *Bryce* ☺

We worked it out with Mr. Forster that Boo could get a free soft drink once a week for the whole school year. Mr. Forster also offered him a free book as long as Boo came in to discuss it. Boo said that sounded too much like school.

Harris came to school late the next day and returned the coins he'd found in a closet. Ashley told me Ms. Prine's eyes lit up like a Christmas tree. I didn't see Harris until lunch. He was eating by himself. He glanced at me, then back at the table.

"We're okay, right?" I said.

He looked like he expected me to smash him. "You mean it?"

"Wasn't your fault." I held out my hand, and he wiped his on his shirt, then shook. "I liked your church, by the way. Other than the service we had in the basement."

He smiled.

"What's going to happen to your brother?"

Harris shrugged. "Mom and Dad are ticked. But Mr. Forster said he wouldn't press charges."

Carlos, who was Lollapawinner88, knew most every screen name. "Sure miss the Red Room."

"Do you know who PingPongU was?" I said.

"That's easy," Carlos said. "Marion Quidley."

My mouth dropped open. *I was talking to Marion?*

"Wait, she was the one who asked who Mr. Forster was."

Carlos shrugged. "A fake out. She wanted to talk anonymously."

CHAPTER 89

❀ Ashley ❀

Bryce and I looked forward to having Mr. Forster back, counting the days until we could ride our ATVs. But he dropped a bomb on us at the grand opening of Juicy Pages. I asked him when his first day back on the job would be, and he gave me a funny look.

"Actually, I'm not coming back," he said. "I know you two put a lot of effort into this, but after talking with my wife, I'm ready for a break."

"But you were made to be a principal—you love being with people."

"I do, but I'm hoping to serve people here. Maybe I'll be back someday, but right now I'm taking some time off from school."

"Does that mean we're stuck with Bookman?" Bryce said.

Mr. Forster laughed. "He's not that bad, is he? From what I've heard, the way you guys handled all this was amazing. You can handle Mr. Bookman."

Something about the walk home made me appreciate my brother more. I'd failed him big-time and he had forgiven me. We'd solved another mystery and had even been helped by Boo Heckler. Even though we couldn't ride our ATVs to school, it was okay. We were the only two people in the world who could be on separate teams and still grow closer.

About the Authors

Jerry B. Jenkins (jerryjenkins.com) is the writer of the Left Behind series. He owns the Jerry B. Jenkins Christian Writers Guild, an organization dedicated to mentoring aspiring authors. Former vice president for publishing for the Moody Bible Institute of Chicago, he also served many years as editor of *Moody* magazine and is now Moody's writer-at-large.

His writing has appeared in publications as varied as *Reader's Digest, Parade, Guideposts,* in-flight magazines, and dozens of other periodicals. Jenkins's biographies include books with Billy Graham, Hank Aaron, Bill Gaither, Luis Palau, Walter Payton, Orel Hershiser, and Nolan Ryan, among many others. His books appear regularly on the *New York Times, USA Today, Wall Street Journal,* and *Publishers Weekly* best-seller lists.

Jerry is also the writer of the nationally syndicated sports story comic strip *Gil Thorp,* distributed to newspapers across the United States by Tribune Media Services.

Jerry and his wife, Dianna, live in Colorado and have three grown sons and three grandchildren.

Chris Fabry is a writer and broadcaster who lives in Colorado. He has written more than 40 books, including collaboration on the Left Behind: The Kids series.

You may have heard his voice on Focus on the Family, Moody Broadcasting, or Love Worth Finding. He has also written for Adventures in Odyssey and Radio Theatre.

Chris is a graduate of the W. Page Pitt School of Journalism at Marshall University in Huntington, West Virginia. He and his wife, Andrea, have been married 22 years and have nine children, a bird, two dogs, and one cat.

RED ROCK MYSTERIES

**WATCH FOR THE NEXT 4 BOOKS
COMING SEPTEMBER 2006!**

WheRe
AdvEnture
beGins
with
a BoOk!

∠LoG oN @
Cool2Read.com